W9-ABA-109

"The missiles are gone . . ."

Visibility was cut to a few feet as the nuclear ship settled on the ocean floor. Agent N3 made radio contact.

"Carter to Wall. How many can you see?"

"Two teams. They've got some kind of sling made of flotation material. They look like six pallbearers."

"Let's hope we can send them to hell."

The clones dropped their missile and turned on him in unison, firing their spears in a cluster.

Carter let the sled slow. Spears clanged off the front of the sled, two bouncing off the nuclear warhead . . .

NICK CARTER IS IT!

"Nick Carter out-Bonds James Bond."
                                    —*Buffalo Evening News*

"Nick Carter is America's #1 espionage agent."
                                    —*Variety*

"Nick Carter is razor-sharp suspense."
                                    —*King Features*

"Nick Carter has attracted an army of addicted readers
. . . the books are fast, have plenty of action and just
the right degree of sex . . . Nick Carter is the American
James Bond, suave, sophisticated, a killer with both the
ladies and the enemy."
                                    —*The New York Times*

FROM THE NICK CARTER KILLMASTER SERIES

DEEP SEA DEATH

KILL MASTER

NICK CARTER

JOVE BOOKS, NEW YORK

"Nick Carter" is a registered trademark of The Condé Nast
Publications, Inc., registered in the United States Patent Office.

KILLMASTER #254: DEEP SEA DEATH

A Jove Book / published by arrangement with
The Condé Nast Publications, Inc.

PRINTING HISTORY
Jove edition / October 1989

All rights reserved.
Copyright © 1989 by The Condé Nast Publications, Inc.
This book may not be reproduced in whole or in part,
by mimeograph or any other means, without permission.
For information address: The Berkley Publishing Group,
200 Madison Avenue, New York, New York 10016.

ISBN: 0-515-10153-2

Jove Books are published by The Berkley Publishing Group,
200 Madison Avenue, New York, New York 10016.
The name "JOVE" and the "J" logo
are trademarks belonging to Jove Publications, Inc.

PRINTED IN THE UNITED STATES OF AMERICA

10 9 8 7 6 5 4 3 2 1

Dedicated to the men and women of the
Secret Services of the
United States of America

ONE

The ten-thousand-ton research vessel *Sir Wilfred Laurier* steamed to the Pearl Harbor entrance by special permission, was intercepted by the nuclear frigate U.S.S. *J. P. Jones* at Hamner Point, exchanged signals, and was escorted past Waipio Peninsula to the Southeast Lock and Pacific Fleet Headquarters. The visitor was an innocuous ship compared to the fighting ships it passed, the best the U.S. Navy had to offer in Pacific waters.

The first person off the ship was Captain Paul Hart, followed by Dr. Julius Flynn and Dr. Barbara Wall. They were met at the dock by a midshipman who saluted and asked them to follow him. He commanded an escort of four naval police, complete with white armbands and helmets. The trio were walked briskly, almost in military cadence, to an impressive white stone building a hundred yards from shore. Not a word was exchanged between the Americans and their Canadian guests.

Barbara Wall thought the whole business of stopping at naval headquarters a waste of time. They were scientists. They carried no armament and were interested only in the exploration of volcanic and sandstone formations in the Hawaiian chain. Typical of the mentality of men playing their games, she thought as she unwillingly trudged along, falling behind. Barbara didn't normally trudge, but she was tired, bored, and indifferent to the need for protocol. Usually her stride was athletic, a match for the body she'd brought to the peak of perfection by pushing it to its physical limit every day. She was a complex woman, one of the best brains of the Foundation for Ocean Research (FOR), a privately endowed underwater and underground research organization under the guidance of the National Research Council in Ottawa, a department of the Canadian government.

In her mind, permission had been sought and granted by their foreign minister during one of his personal visits to the secretary of state in Washington. It had been routine. The countries were the best of friends, about to enter into a trade agreement unprecedented on their side of the Atlantic. All of this—this useless posturing—was a waste of time.

The small group entered the ten-story building, the ensign saluted from corridor to corridor by guards placed at every strategic location. They crowded into a small express elevator at the rear of the building and were whisked to their destination in seconds. The top-floor lobby was about twenty feet square. It contained only a guard post manned by four men and one huge steel door.

The metal door opened with the push of an unseen button, and the Canadians were led past another half-dozen guards to a beautifully scrolled wooden door and into an office that totally surprised Dr. Barbara Wall.

It was huge. One wall, fully forty feet long, looked out over the harbor, commanding a view of most of the ships at anchor. The walls were of expensive cherrywood paneling, with subtly lighted reproductions of French masters gracing them. The furniture, in two groupings, were of the finest leather, and the one functional piece, a highly polished desk of simple lines, placed in front of the expanse of glass, held a single orange folder. A phone was attached to the side of the desk at the occupant's right hand. He rose as they entered.

Only one word described Admiral Charles "Cube" Brenner. In Barbara Wall's opinion, the word was "dynamic." Energy seemed to crackle from the man like static electricity. True to the nickname bestowed on him by his men, he was built like a football tackle, scaled down to about five feet ten. His hair was no more than half an inch long, blond turning to white, a contrast to the deeply tanned face that made his blue eyes seem even brighter.

Barbara's first impression was of a stern man, a disciplinarian, but as she watched him, totally absorbed, the leatherlike skin of his face crinkled at the eyes and his smile made up for the almost chilly reception they'd received thus far.

"Welcome. Please sit and make yourselves comfortable," he said.

When they were seated and stewards had served them steaming coffee in mugs emblazoned with the admiral's personal insignia, he looked from one to the other with his remarkable ice-blue eyes. She noticed he didn't waste time with introductions. He knew who they were and they knew who he was. But she was wrong if she thought his interest was casual. He made sure they knew he had a thorough background on them.

"Let me make sure my information is correct," he said, turning to the captain first. "Captain Paul Edward Hart. Commodore of the RCN, retired, presented the Navy Cross by my government for action in the Sea of Japan during the Korean War. Took command of the newly commissioned oceanography ship *Sir Wilfred Laurier* exactly fifteen months ago.''

Captain Hart sat, surprised at the detail and the total recall, his great frame immobile in the chair he challenged with his bulk. He was in dress whites, his captain's stripes in gold, four rows of ribbons a splash of color on his left breast. His round face was almost covered with a full but neatly trimmed beard.

"Dr. Julius Caesar Flynn, bachelor of science from McGill University in Montreal in biology, master's degree from the University of Toronto in archaeology, took your doctorate in oceanography at Harvard," the admiral went on. "Worked on the *Titanic* project, headed up an oceanography project last year in the Arctic in liaison with the Cousteau group. Married with three children, all named after biblical characters, a concession to your fully ordained spouse."

Barbara had never seen Flynn's mouth gaping in wonder at anything. In fact, she'd never seen him fully surprised before, even at discoveries they'd made together hundreds of feet beneath the sea.

"It shouldn't have surprised me to find Dr. Barbara Alice Wall on this expedition. Doctorate in anthropology from Stamford, distinguished by several notable expeditions," the military man went on. "I was surprised to learn that you are a black belt in karate and can bench press more than double your body weight. Is anthropology that strenuous, Dr. Wall?" he asked.

It was the first time any of the three Canadians had a chance to get a word in. Barbara was taken aback. She hadn't known Julius's middle name was Caesar or that anyone knew her middle name. It didn't appear on any of her records, not even through her distinguished academic career.

"Apparently no one informed you of our specific mission, Admiral," she replied. "We are interested in the archaeology of cave dwellers as much as in our ocean research. Many islands built up from both volcanic rock and sandstone contain huge caverns. Some were occupied thousands of years ago, long before these islands were populated. I'm surprised you didn't learn that for yourself when you were marooned less than five hundred miles from here," she went on. "You lost a ship you attempted to salvage from a battle in the Sea of Japan about the time Captain Hart was on active service. I understand you were the only survivor and spent a number of weeks alone on an island rife with caves and caverns."

The admiral grinned at her, then let out a guffaw that shook the walls. An officer and two NCOs looked in, guns drawn. They retreated as fast as they'd reacted.

"Touché, Dr. Wall. I'll let you in on a secret. The most feared admiral in the Pacific command is a claustrophobic. You'd never get me down in a submarine. The best I could manage was in a fire control center deep in the bowels of a cruiser. I didn't explore the caves—not my idea of a good time."

The ice was broken. The battle lines that might have been drawn between a military man who had to conduct all his business in strictest secrecy, and the group of civilians who would be nosing around his private preserves, were never permitted to materialize.

"We'll try to keep out of your way, Admiral," Flynn assured him. "We intend to drop anchor at every piece of rock within a thousand miles of here and explore it for caverns. You'll probably be completely unaware of us."

"It's not that simple, Dr. Flynn," Brenner said. "My radar picks up a flyspeck on the ocean within three hundred miles of here. My fleet air arm flies sorties and training exercises over the whole area you will cover. We'll know where you are at all times.''

Barbara listened to the words and sensed his specially trained mind at work. Her long-held animosity toward things military surfaced briefly. She didn't like to have her every move watched. It was bad enough that satellites tracked them when time could be spared from other reconnaissance. That modern technology could track them at will was disquieting for a scientist who liked to feel that she was miles from civilization looking backward through the centuries at signposts left by ancient peoples.

''You'll pardon my asking, Admiral,'' Captain Hart said, ''but the yard seems to be on a full alert, almost a wartime footing. I've been here before. It's not the same today.''

The admiral was quiet for a few minutes. Apparently Hart had struck a nerve and the admiral was trying to decide on his best course of action. ''We have a top-secret ship in dry dock here for a final fitting. Our enemies would dearly love to get a look at her.'' It was obvious he wasn't about to reveal more. Instead, he got up and pressed a button on the wall in front of them. A map of his command rolled silently from a concealed slot in the ceiling.

''I'd appreciate it if you would stay away from this area until my new charge is out of the area,'' he said, indicating the island to the west, out past the Kure Atoll.

''That's where your new craft will conduct its trials?'' Captain Hart asked. ''Isn't that usually classified?''

''Right. They'll be under sealed orders. But my guess is that they'll be out past Kure.''

''We're following Necker Ridge to the southeast,'' Dr. Flynn said. ''The first rocky outcroppings we'll be exploring are to the west of Horizon Tablemount. We won't be within four hundred miles of the Kure Atoll.''

"Then I don't see any problems," the admiral said, walking purposefully back to his desk. Apparently the interview was over. By the time the three scientists were out the door, stewards had been in, cleared away the mugs and trays, and the office was as spotless as when the admiral had reported in that morning.

"Give me some slack," Flynn said as he lowered himself to a shelf of rock at the fourth level. They had entered the cave four hours earlier and encountered two underground lakes. By conducting extensive underwater searches, they'd managed to find an outflow that took them to another cavern in each case. They left an orange-colored trailing line behind them, secured at their point of entry.

"What do you say we break for lunch?" Barbara suggested when the five of them were gathered on the shelf of rock.

Three undergraduates, strong young men, accompanied Julius Flynn and Barbara Wall on the descent. It would have been totally dark for the five members of the party except for the long-life lanterns each member of the group carried.

"I'm famished," one of the young men admitted.

He was always famished, Barbara thought. In more ways than one. He was always first to the table. He was the first and only one to approach her on the long sea journey out of Vancouver. And he was the only one to share her bed. Her looks were a trial as well as a blessing. The long blond hair and hazel eyes were a match for the almost perfect body. During her whole academic career she tried to hide her beauty under unattractive clothing and dark-rimmed glasses. Now, a scholar with an established reputation, she had eased up—and it had caught up with her once or twice.

When he'd made his play she'd been bored and the thought of physical pleasure was not far from her mind. His appetite had been voracious. It had happened only once, a weak moment in an otherwise dull trip and an act she wasn't about to repeat. But her refusals hadn't stopped him from trying.

"Let's take a half hour," Flynn agreed. "We could all use a rest."

They had sandwiches in waterproof containers inside their packs and each had a thermos of coffee. Barbara carried a bottle of brandy for emergencies. She'd seen hypothermia rear its ugly head on other expeditions and knew the benefit of the liquor's warmth down a cold gullet. The brandy was in one breast pocket of the waterproof shirt she wore over her wet suit. In the other pocket she carried a reference book she'd written on rare sea creatures.

"I'm surprised this turns you on," Rod Lang said, easing himself down beside her.

"It's what I dream of when I'm on dry land," she said, allowing him a small smile. "When I'm cold and hungry, I dream of dry land."

"That's what I like. A complicated woman," the young man said, maintaining eye contact, not letting her forget their time together.

"You ever get scared?" he asked.

"I used to. My first two or three descents were the hardest, you know, squeezing through a narrow underground river, not knowing what's on the other side, hoping your breathing gear's not going to snag on anything."

"How far down do you figure we are?" he asked.

"My depth meter shows six hundred feet, but that could be out by twenty percent. Let's see," she said, furrowing her brow in thought. "The first drop was about fifty feet.

Hard to figure the first river . . . maybe we dropped another thirty feet to the first big cavern.''

"The cavern was at least a hundred feet high," he offered.

"So that was just a little less than two hundred feet. I figure the first water hole we explored was maybe fifty feet deep and the river we followed dropped another hundred and fifty."

"So that's three-fifty?"

"And the rest following that twisting tunnel three hundred feet down."

"Yeah," he said without enthusiasm. "Crawling on your knees, or on your gut for what seemed like two miles."

"Wish you'd never come?" she asked, half teasing.

"Except for one night. The whole expedition was worth that one night."

"Keep your voice down," she said, elbowing him in the ribs. "You can hear a damned pin drop down here."

"So what? So they all find out. Why deny it?" he asked, catching her eye again and grinning.

God, but I was a damned fool, she thought as she finished her sandwich. She still had half her thermos of coffee and closed the cap before it cooled.

"I still think it's like a miracle to find pockets of air, even huge caverns so far below the ocean surface. It doesn't seem that gravity's at work here at all," he said.

"Water pressure's neutralized by the internal lakes and rivers," she said, adjusting her gear. "Something like the trap under a sink that keeps sewer gasses out. I've seen caverns the size of football fields hundreds of feet below the sea. That's where we've made our best finds."

"Well, this trip has helped me decide on the future.

When I think of being six hundred feet below the surface, my stomach churns. It's scary.''

"Maybe you'll get used to it. Give it another try."

"The last river we descended? The one that was so narrow? I felt myself wedged a couple of times and almost panicked. It's just not for me."

"We were all frightened the first few times," she said, trying to reassure him.

"Do you ever think of what would happen if we lost the guide line?" he asked.

A shiver coursed through her spine. It was the one thing that woke her up screaming out of a deep sleep. If they ever lost their guide line, they'd be dead. No one could remember all the twists and turns made in an underground trek.

"Think about something else," she said.

"Except for you, it's all I think about."

"C'mon, Rod. That night was fun, but it's over. And if you let yourself get freaked about the climbs, you'll be confined to the boat."

"Might not be a bad idea. How many descents have we tried anyway?"

"A dozen."

"And we haven't found a goddamned thing."

"No one ever said that anthropology would be fun all the time," she told him. "Sometimes you go for weeks without finding anything, not so much as a scratch on a wall. Then the first find could be a simple drawing or a whole panorama. That's part of the thrill."

"How the hell did the ancients get down into these caves? We've got the best equipment and it's never easy," he observed, sitting too close to her, making her move to keep her own space. "How'd they stand the cold of the water? How'd they hold their breath through the long, narrow rivers and the deep pools?''

"Who knows? Maybe the caverns shifted. Perhaps they were closer to the surface years ago. That's what makes it so interesting.''

"Interesting." He chewed on the word for a few seconds as if absorbed in private thoughts. "Why do we do it, Barb?''

She hated the "Barb." Especially from a handsome college senior she'd been fool enough to let seduce her in a weak moment. But she thought about the question. "Any answer would sound trite, Rod. 'Because it's there' is as good an answer as any.''

The small cavern trembled for a second or two.

"My God! What the hell was that?" Rod spoke, louder than the whispered conversation he'd had with her.

"This is an active volcanic area," Flynn explained. He'd been in deep discussion with the other two, unaware of their conversation. "You'll get rumbles like that all the time—feel them for hundreds of miles.''

"But one a little worse could close some of the narrow passages we came through," Rod said, genuinely alarmed.

"That's why we had to sign a release," Flynn joked. "No sweat, really. The odds against a real shift are several millions to one.''

While he spoke a rumble more severe than the first shook the walls. Rocks fell on them from above. One hit Rod on the side of the head, knocking him sideways into a deep pool.

Barbara eased herself down and got a hand around his arm. "Pull my other arm!" she yelled at the others.

Flynn and one of the other youths grabbed for her free arm and one of them got Rod by the armpit and dragged him back to the flat rock shelf.

"Is he all right?" Barbara asked.

"Strong pulse," Flynn said. "Probably a concussion. We should get him to the surface in a hurry."

"Not until he comes around. He's got to manage his own scuba gear," she reminded him, examining the wound. It was a deep gash, still bleeding profusely. She reached for her backpack and the waterproof first aid kit she carried.

"What about the rumble—the possible shift?" one of the young men asked. "Do you think we'll have any trouble getting back?"

"The odds are in our favor," Flynn answered solemnly. "I shouldn't have kidded about it. We're okay—really."

Barbara worked on the cut and thought about Flynn's statement. He had to say that. The others were young, inexperienced. They needed all the confidence he could feed them.

"What do you think it was?" the other student asked.

"It could have been anything—a small earthquake, although I hope not, or it could have been a volcanic eruption hundreds of miles away. Or maybe just a simple earth crust shift."

"Why'd you say 'I hope not'?"

"Because there'd be aftershocks."

"What about an explosion?" the first young man asked.

"What the hell would explode around here?" Flynn asked, obviously tired of the questions.

"Well, maybe the U.S. Navy's on a training mission. Or—"

"Forget it," Flynn cut him off. "How's Rod?" he asked Barbara.

"Coming around. We should be able to take him up in a few minutes."

"Where's the trail rope?" the first young men asked as he rose on the ledge, holding his lamp and balancing with one hand on the rock face. "It was tied to me all the way. I just untied it a few minutes ago."

"You idiot!" the other youth cried. "How will we get back now?"

"Cool it, you two. Look around. It's got to be here somewhere," Flynn said.

"It couldn't have gone up by itself," the first youth said, almost in a panic. "It was right beside me here when I was eating."

While they were arguing among themselves, the water in the pool they'd planned to explore after lunch started to change color. From an inky black, broken only by the reflections of their lamps, to gray, then to light yellow.

Several sources of light separated and came upward growing in strength.

"What is it?" Barbara whispered, supporting Rod in front of her. Her back was to the rock wall, the injured man lying against her.

Flynn was speechless for once. The two students were holding their lamps in front of them, shading their eyes, trying to see what was coming at them from the deep.

The lights broke the water and almost blinded them. They backed against the rock wall. Dark shadows emerged from the pool wearing a style of diving gear they had never seen before.

"Who are you?" Flynn asked, finally coming out of his stupor.

The five newcomers still had their self-contained underwater breathing apparatus in their mouths and weird masks covering their faces. They moved their lamps to one side to reveal wicked harpoons in their other hands.

Without a word, the swimmers from the depths squeezed their triggers in unison and the hiss of compressed gas masked the sound of barbed spears churning through soft flesh.

Flynn and the others were flung backward against the cavern wall and crumpled in pools of their own blood, each skewered through the heart, dead before they hit the rock.

A harpoon passed through Rod and struck Barbara Wall, knocking her head against the rock behind her. The pain was excruciating. She'd never felt anything like it. But she was not unconscious. She floated somewhere between the blackness of death and the faint hope of life.

"That all of them?" she heard.

"That's it," a voice above them answered. She was barely conscious of the voice above her, but her questing brain solved the mystery of the disappearing trail rope. They had been attacked from both directions.

"The other team took care of the boat," one of the swimmers said. "It's on the bottom by now. I felt the concussion all the way down here."

"Good. Our job is done. Let's report back to Zendal," the voice above said, fading until she heard nothing.

Slowly the lights disappeared. Everything was total darkness.

She wasn't unconscious. It was just dark. And the pain had lessened; it was more like a deep throbbing than a puncture. She moved Rod away from her on the slippery rock shelf.

She might have been unconscious for a few minutes, but now her senses were alert. The place smelled of death, the sheared-metal smell of blood. Somehow she got her hands behind Rod and pushed. The harpoon came away and she was free. The barbed tip that had passed through Rod had been stopped by her reference book. She figured she'd have a bruise the size of a football on her chest, but that appeared to be the worst of her injuries. Her head had been protected by her wet suit hood.

Rod slid into the cold water at her feet and she almost screamed out for him as he entered his watery grave. But she couldn't scream. They, whoever they might be, could come back.

Barbara felt along the rock face and slipped in a pool of liquid. She scraped a knee and ripped her wet suit as her hand found the end of a pole. She felt along the shaft until her hand found Flynn's body.

She continued her search. The other two were gone; they had probably slipped into the same watery grave.

She was alone.

TWO

Nick Carter's room at the Sheraton Kaanapali looked out over the Pacific toward Lanai across the Auau Channel. He'd been there a week, about as much R & R as his agile mind was able to take between jobs before he began to itch for the excitement of another assignment. The week had been uneventful. While many of the women at the hotel had tried to catch his eye, this time he hadn't winked back, a state of affairs his boss, David Hawk, wouldn't have believed.

But that was about to change. Earlier in the week a friend had introduced him to a private club, one with a license to run its own casino for members only. The only woman who had interested him was a member. As he stood in front of a mirror straightening his black tie, he felt a surge of adrenaline at the anticipation of the chase.

A dark-haired man was reflected back at him, the face ruggedly handsome, the dark eyes hinting at life fully experienced. He smiled as he thought of an interesting night ahead at the green tables of the casino, the intriguing woman, and the pleasure that would inevitably follow.

The club was almost empty. It was luxurious in its own understated way. No glitz and noise here as in Vegas. The

17

few people milling around were in formal dress. The minimum bet was twenty-five dollars. He consulted his Rolex. It was still early, but it didn't matter. He decided to play blackjack until she showed.

Carter preferred to play one-on-one with the dealer and figured he might just have enough time for the hundreds of hands needed to guarantee success. He requested the table be posted at a hundred-dollar minimum and placed twenty hundred-dollar bills on the table. The dealer stacked twenty black chips in front of him. Carter bet one.

The dealer's hands moved quickly. They both had "breaking" hands, between twelve and sixteen. He decided to stand pat, knowing the dealer had no such choice. The dealer lost and payed off. Carter, the premier agent of AXE, an ultrasecret intelligence organization set up years earlier at the request of the president, signaled that the bet would stand.

Carter ran his streak of wins to six. He bet three chips on the third hand, four on the fourth, four on the fifth, and five on the sixth, a progression system he'd been taught by Mike Goodman at the Dunes in Las Vegas a few years earlier. The game continued at lightning speed and started to draw spectators.

While the pit boss offered free drinks, changed the cards frequently, and even resorted to changing the dealer—anything to stop the bleeding—the beautiful woman Carter had seen earlier sat at the table and spread a handful of green chips in front of her.

The pit boss sighed, his relief evident. He couldn't have asked for more if the woman had been employed by him. Languidly she ordered a champagne cocktail and coaxed the winner to have the same.

Carter was not out to break the casino. His real objec-

tive had been the lovely creature now sitting beside him.
She placed a chip in the rectangle in front of her.

She was one of the most stunning women he'd ever
seen. She was a raven-haired beauty with ivory skin. Her
eyes, like his, were dark brown, almost black. Her mouth
was perfection and her high cheekbones hinted of a native
heritage. And if her face wasn't enough to attract men, her
figure was spectacular.

"This is a hundred minimum, madam," the dealer said,
using his most deferential manner.

She graced him with a dazzling smile as she pushed a
stack of green chips on the rectangle in front of her.

He dealt two hands and waited.

The woman looked at her cards and slipped them beneath her pile of chips. Carter had a five and six against
the dealer's five showing, an ideal time to double up. He
added seven chips to the bet.

The dealer flipped a nine on the five and six, giving
Carter twenty. He waved off other cards. By this time a
good dozen people stood behind him, whispering and
pointing.

The dealer flipped his down card. It was a six, giving
him an eleven. Without hesitation he dealt himself another
card as the spectators held their breath.

A seven. Carter had won again.

The dealer paid him the fourteen chips and flipped over
the woman's cards. Seventeen. He raked in the pile of
green chips and waited for their bets.

"Damn!" she said. "This is so boring."

"And what would you prefer?" Carter asked.

"A walk around the grounds. A sail in the moonlight.
Anything but this."

It was a test and he knew it. No respectable player left a
table when he was hot, winner of almost three thousand

dollars within minutes. And it wasn't the amount. Players bet more, won and lost more. It was the professional way he'd done it.

"I'm Natalie Foreman," she said, flashing her magnificent long-lashed brown eyes at him. "And you are . . . ?"

"Carter. Nick Carter. And why don't we try the gardens?" he suggested.

"Cash me in," he said, turning to the pit boss. A signal passed between them. Carter knew that he could have gone on to hurt the house badly. The pit boss was as aware as he. In the parlance of the game he was a "tough" player. Apparently some things were more important than money.

The spectators gasped when they realized the winner was about to quit. It just wasn't done. With the mystique associated with winning and losing, they chose to believe he could win at will. It never occurred to them he'd give up thousands for a woman.

When they were in his room, the walk through the gardens forgotten, she put the question to him, the question everyone at the casino wanted to ask. "Why quit when you were ahead?"

"I've gambled all over the world: Mombassa, Macao, London, the Bahamas, Las Vegas. The tables will always be there."

"But you could have won thousands."

"I'd much rather be here with you."

"How gallant," she said, smiling, accepting the champagne he offered. "Gallant and gracious," she added.

"Just practical," he said. She'd never know how much truth was in that statement. Carter led the kind of life in which money was useless. He was seldom a week or two without an assignment. When he needed money and equipment on the job, it was provided. His pay was not excessive, but it had a way of piling up while he was on some of the longer projects. He had his restored Jaguar XKE and his brownstone in Georgetown. When he wanted diversion he always had enough money, and windfalls like tonight's came along every so often to sweeten the pot. It was the kind of life few would understand. Even among those in his profession he was unique. And he was the best. When he was plying his trade, every ounce of his energy and considerable intelligence was exploited to the maximum. But when he played, it was with a flair, with panache. He was one of a rare breed, a dying breed.

Carter put down his fluted glass. He walked up to Natalie and gently lifted her chin. As his lips met hers, he heard the muted sound of her glass hitting the deep pile carpet.

His hands slid around her and inside her clinging, open-backed dress. He drew her closer to him. She came eagerly, the heat of her mouth a fair gauge of her intentions as their tongues intertwined.

He slipped one thin strap off her shoulder and then the other. As he moved slightly away, the garment fell to her hips. She was wearing nothing beneath it and her breasts jutted proudly as he looked down on the kind of perfection that never failed to fill him with awe at such beauty.

The dress was smooth against her skin and without the support of the straps it slithered past her hips and came to rest on the floor.

He stood back while she assumed a model's pose, hands on hips, shoulders back, raising the cones of her breasts, hipshot, one leg taking most of her weight.

She wore only a pair of bikini panties and high-heeled gold sandals. The effect would have been ludicrous if she hadn't been so incredibly beautiful.

He moved back to her and swept her off her feet, claiming her lips again with his. The heat of her brought him to a level of passion he had a hard time controlling. He'd have to go very slowly or he'd make a fool of himself, a schoolboy declaring his first time.

He put her on the bed and lay beside her, running his hands over her body, sliding the wisp of nylon down her legs, feeling her nipples harden under his touch, kissing her from neck to thighs until she moaned, tearing at his clothing. He had to help her. She managed the jacket, the tie, and the shirt, but he had to roll backward while she pulled off his pants. It was done in seconds but they seemed to have been apart for minutes.

She was more than just a beautiful face and a beautiful body. Her skin was taut, her muscles lithe, her strength well above average. The thought was a fleeting message, but it also suggested she would have stamina. He deliberately controlled himself to make sure the night was memorable, and for his efforts he received whispered demands and strong arms pulling him on top of her.

He'd been ready for some time but he'd planned to draw it out. It was just past eleven. They had not turned on the lights, but the moon was full and it bathed them in a creamy glow. She smelled of bath soap and something else, the unmistakable musk given off by a woman who is ready, past ready, frantic for fulfillment.

She felt for him and her soft hand was like a live wire. She guided him to her and moved up to meet him, kissing him, moaning deep in her throat as she took all of him deep inside her.

He tried to hold her still, to savor the moment, but she writhed beneath him, forced him to move with her, brought the friction of their joining to a maximum, a force that he could not deny.

With a roar of passion, he clamped his arms around her

and held her tightly in his powerful grasp while he acceded to her unspoken command.

She moaned, sometimes gasped, and finally screamed as he brought her from one climax to another. She had demanded his best and she was going to get it. She had provided the perfect vessel, and Carter was determined she'd never again have to wonder what fulfillment meant.

The journey seemed endless. Her stamina, as he'd suspected, was a match for his own. She moved with him through one last long climax that brought them to a peak seldom reached, a peak that brought them the seldom-quaffed nectar meant for the gods.

When at last it was over, they clung to each other, she whispering words of endearment in his ear that he couldn't really hear, he running his hands softly over her until she was back to mortal plains, back in the room, back on the sheets that had been their passage to heaven.

When they parted, she saw his cigarettes on a night table and asked for one. He lit two of the custom-blended cigarettes with his gold Dunhill and passed one to her.

She leaned on an elbow above him, looking at the muscular torso. She leaned across him from time to time to flick the ash from her cigarette, and each time the frown deepened on her face. "The scars," she said at last. "An accident? No," she corrected herself. "More than that. Some are older than others. Some are puckered like small rosebuds; some are shiny like knife marks. But none of these were made by a medical man." She hesitated for a moment as if afraid to ask. "Who the hell are you, Nick Carter?"

It was a question he had to evade all too often. "I'm a foreign correspondent most of the time. Amalgamated Press and Wire Services. I work out of Washington when they can find me." It wasn't entirely a lie. Amalgamated Press and Wire Services was the front for AXE headquarters in Washington, D.C., and for its many offices around the world.

"Come on. Foreign correspondents don't get banged up as much as this."

The phrasing was pregnant with innuendo, but he decided to let it go. "I did some soldiering before I took up journalism," he lied. His sixth sense was taking over. He'd been too relaxed in the islands for the past week. What the hell had happened to his training? This could be an enemy agent pumping him with seemingly innocent questions. Enough innocent answers and his enemies would have a pattern that could tell them more than AXE wanted them to know.

His thoughts were interrupted by the phone. In the quiet of the room it sounded like a fire alarm. He picked it up and walked to the far corner of the room, dragging the long cord after him.

"Nick? It's Ginger."

He cupped his hand around the mouthpiece. "Yes?"

"Someone with you?"

"You could say that."

"Ah, romantic Hawaii . . ." She hesitated a second, not wanting her true feelings to come to the surface. She was David Hawk's right hand, and she and Carter had become involved briefly many years earlier but realized the liaison was foolish and dangerous in their line of work. "Hawk is tied up in Bangkok. We lost an agent last night."

"And Hawk went to check it out? Why didn't Smitty go? He's head of Operations—it's his job."

"You haven't heard. Smitty's in the hospital. Some kind of virus."

It was unusual for Hawk to leave Washington. Carter

knew it would take something like Rupert Smith being seriously ill to get him away from AXE headquarters at Dupont Circle. Losing an agent was always difficult. Usually loose ends had to be tied up and new assignments made.

Carter didn't ask who they had lost. It almost invariably turned out to be someone he knew, someone he'd worked with. And right now he didn't want to know. He'd learned that pain dulled his responses and mourning eroded concentration.

"I presume this call is important," he muttered.

"Yes, it is, Nick. Very," she said. "A Canadian research team is missing. They were granted permission to explore uncharted islands around Hawaii."

"Details?" he asked, keeping the conversation at his end to a minimum.

"A fairly large expedition. Ten-thousand-ton ship, crew of ten. They have two experts on the expedition, specialists in anthropology, archaeology, and some oceanography thrown in there somewhere. Three or four undergraduates with them."

"Their mission?" he asked.

"Simple enough. Hunt for extensive caverns in sandstone rock formation in the Pacific. They've got our secretary of state's blessing."

"Equipment?" he asked.

"That's the strange thing. A ten-thousand-ton oceanography vessel, the *Sir Wilfred Laurier*, recently commissioned, named after one of their earlier prime ministers."

Carter noticed that Natalie was in the bathroom with the door closed. He faintly heard the sound of a shower. "Even a large ship like theirs could easily be lost in the Pacific," he said. "What's the excitement?"

"They made a courtesy call to Admiral Brenner at

Pacific Fleet Headquarters only days ago. At first he was able to track them on his radar from headquarters, then they lost it. The admiral issued orders for every ship or plane in their vicinity to report their position.''

"I see what you mean. With all the training sorties they make, hundreds of sightings should have been made. Couldn't we reach them by radio?''

"Dead silence. It's as if they disappeared from the face of the earth.''

"Did Hawk leave any instructions?''

"Not very specific. He wanted you because you're close to the scene. Howard's going to be your control on this one.''

Howard Schmidt was their expert on identification and their specialist with gadgets. He was completely gadget-crazy and tried to press his latest inventions on Carter at every opportunity. Some of them were pretty weird, but sometimes they'd proved to be invaluable. For all his eccentricities, Schmidt was one of Carter's real friends in what was in truth a very lonely profession.

"What's Howard got in mind?'' Carter asked.

"He's already outbound from the San Diego naval base in one of the merchant marine's fastest freighters. He's got some kind of boat he wants you to try out on this one.''

"He never gives up, does he. What am I supposed to do in the meantime?''

"Take a plane to Honolulu. A navy escort will take you to Admiral Brenner. He's agreed to outfit you for cavern exploration and drop you at the last known location of the expedition.''

"And how is Howard supposed to catch up with me?''

"He's sent along a couple of gadgets by navy jet. They should be waiting for you in the admiral's office.''

"For a small operation, Howard's pulling out all the

stops," Carter observed. "These people could be in a sheltered harbor. They might not want to be found."

"I know. And Howard could be blowing our budget on a wild-goose chase."

"While the cat's away . . ." Carter mused. "It's okay. The poor devil's trapped in his basement office most of the time and we probably don't appreciate him enough. Let him have his fun this time. It could be interesting.

"One last thing," he said. "Send out word for Stonewall Kuhuhu. I used to do some diving with him. He owns his own scuba shop on Waikiki Beach. Get clearance for him and have him meet me at Brenner's office."

"Can do. Good luck, Nick," Ginger said. She always left him with that as her last thought. They both knew that he hadn't survived longer than any of them by luck. He was the best, physically and mentally, of any agent in the West, and better than anyone the enemy had thrown against him.

In a few hours he'd know if the challenge was worthy of his talent.

THREE

The office on the top floor was filled with officers in dress whites. Stewards with trays of drinks circulated among the group. It was significant to Carter that they were all men, all full commanders or higher in rank, and all tight-lipped. A civilian was totally out of place. The admiral solved the problem of privacy by taking Carter into a small office adjoining his.

The man seemed to fill the room with his presence. He stood, a block of granite, his face totally devoid of emotion. This was going to be one of those military minds who hated dealing with any kind of covert intelligence problem, who treated people like Carter with contempt, Carter thought. But this wasn't going to be a major problem. It was too simple for that. A group of scientists had disappeared. They were probably in some secluded cove, shielded from radar, not programmable on scanners from aircraft passing over.

"This should be simple for you, Carter," Admiral Brenner said. "I've read your file, or the little I could get on you. Impressive. Can't understand why they'd put you on to something like this."

So Carter had underestimated the admiral. He usually

didn't prejudge anyone. "What's the occasion for the party?" he asked.

The admiral's expression told the story. He was obviously caught between total "eyes only" secrecy, and a compulsion to boast about his new acquisition. "You've got all the top clearances," he said, "so I guess there's no harm in telling you. We've completed the final fitting for the U.S.S. *Lance*."

"Our identification expert gave me a rundown on her last month. An unbelievable piece of machinery," Carter said.

"We don't have pieces of machinery now, Carter," Brenner said, softening his tone. "She's an electronic marvel. A destroyer carrying six nuclear missiles, two dozen mounts for ship-to-air missiles, electronic detection devices that go beyond advertised state of the art."

"And she's going out for trials?"

"Tomorrow. She'll be under sealed orders direct from the Chief of Staff's office. I'm pretty sure I know where they'll send her and it's not where the Canadians are missing. My guess is they're sending her out beyond Kure Atoll in the Midway Island chain. She'll be alone, but we can monitor her from here."

"I wish you well, Admiral. What arrangements have you made for me?"

"We gave the Canadians royal treatment. The *J. P. Jones*, one of our nuclear frigates, escorted them in and out," Brenner said, drinking the last of the glass he'd been carrying. "Their captain, Paul Hart, and our Commander Straight exchanged a few stories. Straight knows as much as anyone about where they were heading and has our last fix on them. He'll take you to the area."

"I asked my people to contact a local man to assist me."

"Mr. Kuhuhu is aboard the *J. P. Jones*. All your gear is stowed and they're ready to go when you are," the admiral said, turning to the door and leading the way back to his office.

The noise level dropped a decibel or two, and most eyes turned to their commanding officer. He led Carter to a tall, thin man in the far corner. A group around Commander Straight broke up and drifted off as the two men approached.

"Commander Straight, Nicholas Carter," Brenner said, his voice strong. The introductions were almost barked out in the babbles that surrounded them. "You've both got your orders. I suggest you get to it," he said as he turned on his heel.

"That's plain enough," Straight said. He leaned down to a side table and deposited his almost filled glass. "Let's get the hell out of here, Carter. You've given me an excuse to get away from some damned boring duty."

"And replaced it with a boring trip along Necker Ridge."

"It's never boring when the steel of my ship is under my feet, Carter. Obviously you're not a seafaring man."

"I've had my share of time at sea."

"Just who are you? Some kind of spook? What's so important about this group?"

"That's three questions, Commander. First, I'm just a troubleshooter from Washington," Carter said, smiling innocently. "I do my job and stay clear of politics. Last, the group was given permission by our secretary of state to explore some of our territory. It seems he feels some kind of responsibility for their safety."

They'd been walking from the headquarters building to the slip where the U.S.S. *J. P. Jones* was berthed. She was sleek, looked fast, and gave the impression she could take care of herself in any kind of action with fair odds.

They were piped aboard. Straight introduced him to his

first officer and disappeared to change into his working clothes. "Take Mr. Carter below to Mr. Kuhuhu. He'll want to inspect his gear," he said as he left.

Stonewall Kuhuhu was sitting in the middle of an audience of enthralled swabbies. The off-duty sailors were bug-eyed at the stories the seasoned islander was telling them about the women of the islands and how they made love. He was one of the most accomplished storytellers Carter had ever met and the biggest liar. He was a coffee-colored man with the build of a weight lifter, his face a stage on which his emotions played a full repertoire, his hair shoulder length, jet black and wavy. His eyes were dark like Carter's, but they were surrounded with crinkled skin that could have only been the product of thousands of smiles and a lot of hours in the sun. He had no worry lines.

The old friends embraced in the fashion of the islands where emotions were never hidden. "Man, haven't seen you since that damned old shark near took off my leg," Kuhuhu said, displaying the scars where the teeth had ripped at the muscle. "Where the hell you been?"

"I've been here and there, old friend. Let's check out our equipment. We can talk later."

Carter followed Kuhuhu through a watertight door and along a companionway to the rear of the ship. In a square steel enclosure at the stern, the navy people had set out an oversize rubber dinghy for them complete with twin seventy-five-horse Johnsons.

"What about climbing gear?" Carter asked.

Kuhuhu pulled the end of a tarpaulin aside and revealed as much equipment as they would need, everything similar to the gear used by mountain climbers, except for the clothes. They had wet suits and skintight underwear to go with it. The gear included a block and tackle.

"What's that for?" Carter asked.

"Better than camouflage. I'll show you when we get there. Take a look at the special package from Washington," Kuhuhu suggested.

To one side, a four-by-four box was unopened. A waterproof delivery sleeve was glued to the top. Howard Schmidt had sent a package already. How he'd managed to get it there so fast, the man from AXE couldn't imagine. Although, through Hawk, Schmidt had access to some high-powered connections.

Carter slit the box open with a knife Kuhuhu freed from the belt around the loose robe he wore. The powerful islander was barefoot as usual.

A note was enclosed in the plastic sleeve.

Nick

This should hold you until I get there with some better equipment. Your weapons are part of the consignment, as usual. I've included my new scuba experimental toy and an earth station. Just off the experimental bench back at Dupont. Don't let anyone get his hands on it. Instructions are included with both. Don't get yourself in any trouble. I'll be there in a couple of days.

Howard

Good old Mother Howard, the provider and the worrier. Carter examined the box for his weapons. His 9mm Luger, Wilhelmina, an old friend he'd used to get out of more scrapes than he could remember, was in her usual leather holster. The long thin stiletto he'd named Hugo was encased in its chamois sheath. He pulled it out and examined the blade. It was clean and razor sharp. Last, he looked over an object no larger than a small lime, a lethal bomb he frequently taped to an inner thigh like a third testicle. The Luger and the stiletto had been with him for years; the bomb was usually left at the scene where he'd used it, two halves rolling on a foreign floor, the lethal gas deadly to anyone who took one whiff. Sometimes, when it was imperative to take prisoners for interrogation, he used a gas bomb designed to render enemies unconscious.

In recent years Schmidt had included a pocket-sized leather case that contained syringes and three kinds of drugs, one to knock out a subject, one to extract the truth from unwilling enemies, and the third to complete a sanction as quietly and quickly as possible.

He put the weapons aside. He felt naked without them, but they'd be donning wet suits soon and he'd probably have to take them in a waterproof backpack.

The new scuba gear was surprisingly small, but it lived up to its acronym: self-contained underwater breathing apparatus—scuba. Instead of a tank of compressed gas, an arrangement of tubes and valves, and a mouthpiece, the new scuba gimmick was a stainless steel tube about four inches long. It had a rubber band around it and another note from Schmidt:

Pull out the black plastic oval in the center of the tube. Use it as a mouthpiece and bite down on it. You'll have ten minutes of air. Try not to use it at extreme depths.

Typical Schmidt magic, Carter thought as the big islander next to him examined the second of the new scuba tubes AXE's inventive genius had sent.

Another package of oiled brown paper contained a group of triangular pieces of metal, an electronic box, and a power pack. It was also ringed by a rubber band and a note. Carter began to feel like a schoolboy being led around by the nose.

If your addled brain can cope with this, we can communicate when I get close to you. It's my new earth station. The triangles interlock to make a dish about a foot in diameter. Push the sensor through the middle of the dish and plug it into the electronic control. You'll see three dials on the control: direction, volume, and push-to-talk. The power pack has its own connector jack and the black box has a clearly marked power plug. Don't let the power source fall into the wrong hands. It's nuclear and totally classified. No one but Hawk and I know about it so far. It will be useful to power many new tools for us in future.

Carter read the note again and put a match to both notes. The embers had just disappeared when the commander showed up.

"What's that gadget?" he asked, reaching for the unassembled earth station.

"How did the box get to us?" Carter countered, making no effort to let the commander see the various parts.

"You must have clout at the highest levels. It was flown over in a prototype B-2 bomber. We've never seen one here and the field was cleared of all personnel while it landed and took off," Straight said, a measure of respect in his voice. "Now, what the hell is that thing?"

"It's as classified as the bomber, Commander. I'm not supposed to show it to anyone. But you've got the right to know something of what you're carrying," Carter conceded. "It's experimental. A complete land station. With this I can raise my people from anywhere on earth."

"Why don't the military have it?"

"They probably will. Most of our new gadgets end up with the military in time." Carter wasn't always crazy about using Schmidt's new toys, preferring to handle most situations as he always had, but he was proud of his friend's genius and wasn't about to see it compromised in any way.

"What are the steel bars?" Straight asked, reaching for Kuhuhu's.

The big islander moved a shoulder an inch or two to put the scuba device out of reach.

"It's our scuba gear for emergencies," Carter admitted.

Straight curled a lip in disgust. "So you don't trust me. All right. I'll get you in as close as I can and that's it for us. Come to the chart room," he told Carter.

The commander unrolled a four-by-four navigation chart. "The last location we have on them was latitude 19 degrees 13 minutes south of Capricorn, longitude 172 degrees 47 minutes west of Greenwich. They planned to follow the Marcus Necker Seamount Chain first, a shelf that stretches hundreds of miles to the southwest."

"What's your private guess, Commander?" Carter asked. The two were on a totally formal footing now. Carter could see the man's point of view. No captain liked to have secrets withheld from him on his own ship. And this captain knew the stranger he'd been ordered to help had clout that reached far beyond his circles. Too bad. It happened all too often and made the job one that kept Carter alone much of the time.

"My guess is they're sitting drinking tea, or whatever Canadians drink, and sunning themselves in the lee of some uncharted rock out there."

"How much fuel can you manage for me?"

"We've got some gadgets of our own, Carter. But we're not so damned closemouthed about them," Straight said, his attitude bitter by this time. "We'll drop you off close to the coordinates. We'll lower a thousand-gallon fuel drum to the sea floor with a floating filler nozzle. The damned thing looks like an albatross floating in the chop.''

"Good enough. I noticed the dinghy had pressure fuel tanks for a two-day trip. We'll use the storage tank as our base.''

He returned to Kuhuhu and found the big man suiting up in his thermal long johns and wet suit. The waters were warm around the islands, but the undersea lakes and rivers they'd encounter could be extremely cold.

Carter stripped to the skin and taped Pierre—his longtime name for the tiny bombs—to the inside of his leg before donning the long underwear.

"Hold it a minute," he said, looking at the small scuba tube. "Strap the tube inside your thigh before you put on your suit.''

"Why, Nick? It goin' to be uncomfortable there.''

"Just do it, Stonewall. Have I ever steered you wrong?''

"Not yet, my man. But all the gods say you can't be right all the time.''

The swells close to the hunk of rock where Straight dropped them were about six feet high, no problem for the oversize dinghy but enough to make their progress less than ten knots. The U.S.S. *J. P. Jones* steamed out of sight, leaving them alone in an empty sea. It was close to noon. The sun overhead was relentless, so the two men wore floppy white canvas hats to protect themselves. Carter was beginning to wish they'd waited to change into wet suits when they found a landfall.

The fake albatross floated beside them. Carter took a bearing in two easily recognizable rocky outcroppings you couldn't really call islands to mark the spot in his memory, and pressed the electric starter button.

The twin Johnsons roared to life. He switched to forward drive and gave the twin motors a quarter throttle. "We'll circle below these two hunks of rock before we take off on our search pattern," he shouted into Kuhuhu's ear over the roar of the motors. "They could be deceiving. Rocky outcroppings like these could have caverns in them thousands of feet below the surface."

The big Hawaiian seemed content to let Carter make all the decisions. While the Killmaster steered them to one of the towers of rock, Kuhuhu broke out two anchors, old Davenports that looked as if they'd seen plenty of hard use, and prepared to lash one to the bow rail and one to the stern. They weren't about to find a beachhead on this pile of rock.

Both men donned their gear. The scuba apparatus was all of a piece, lashed to webbing that also held their backpacks. When they entered the water, they were about as streamlined as they could be. They'd have to present a minimum profile if they were to traverse some of the underwater rivers and narrow passages they'd find.

The waters of Necker Ridge were warm. With Carter leading the way, they swam from the anchored dinghy around each of the rocky outcroppings without finding anything. They examined every angle of rock to a depth of fifty feet without spotting so much as a ten-foot indentation.

On the surface, bobbing beside the boat, Kuhuhu pulled out his mouthpiece. "What now?" he asked.

Carter scrambled over the side. "We explore everything by line of sight. There must be ten or twelve uncharted rock formations jutting up around here. We record them on our charts, make a square search, then fan out further each day."

"With only a two-day supply of fuel, we can't take in the whole Necker Chain."

"Let's hope we get lucky. The navy radar should be

first rate. They have to be around here, somewhere in our range."

"Why don't we try that new gadget of yours, try to raise them by radio?"

"The navy's had a constant signal sent out to them since they disappeared. All they got was dead air."

"So which hunk of rock are you heading for?"

Carter started the motors and pointed to his right. "That one's the biggest. Let's try it."

He brought the dinghy up to about fifteen knots and headed for the towering hunk of rock, going with the swells at an angle. The wind was at their backs. They'd reach the island, if you could call it that, on the weather side.

It took all of fifteen minutes. The weather side was all rock reaching to the sky. The sea had eaten away at the rock, carving a concave slope at the base where the rock was softest. The granite slabs were unchanged from the moment they'd been thrust from the sea. It looked impossible to climb, offered no landfall, and wasn't even occupied by sea birds.

"I'm going to circle the whole island before we get wet," Carter shouted in Kuhuhu's ear.

The lee side was a surprise. As they rounded a wind-whipped corner of rock, palm trees waved their fronds at them and a small sandy beach beckoned.

"What do you think?" Kuhuhu asked.

"We pull the dinghy onshore and explore around the whole rock to a depth of fifty feet, maybe more. If they've found an entrance to a cavern, they'd be on the weather side."

They made twenty-five knots on the lee side and were on the beach, pulling the rubber dinghy up the soft sand within minutes.

"We'll do a quick search of the weather side, then we'll come back here and cook up something," Carter suggested. "I'll be ready for one of your island specialties as soon as we've swept this one clean."

With flippers making a weird pattern in the sand, the two men entered the water and started around a rocky outcropping back to the weather side. The island was about a mile around at sea level. After one circuit and a thorough search they'd be tired and hungry and would probably call it a day.

Swimming strongly, his flippers pushing him through the water, a lantern in one hand and a harpoon in the other, Carter led the way around the island at a depth of about twenty feet. He could see every angle of the rock face to a depth of thirty feet. Kuhuhu swam behind, a second pair of eyes, making sure the Killmaster didn't miss an opening that could spell the end of their search.

They circumnavigated the island to the lee side and turned back, tracing their path but at a depth of fifty feet.

Carter was the first to spot it. Where the yellow light of their lanterns bounced off the rock, nothing reflected from the dark hole in the rock. Carter swam closer. An opening showed up as a black void against the shining rock.

The two men stopped in front of the hole. Carter motioned for Kuhuhu to follow.

Their lights showed them a cave filled with water. It was twenty feet wide at the opening and spread to forty feet or more at the sides.

At first the cave appeared to go nowhere, then Carter spotted a slope and his light showed an opening at least ten feet wide that gradually sloped downward.

Kuhuhu was eager to explore right away, but Carter held him back with a wave of his hand. He signaled for a

detailed search of the first opening before they proceeded
into unknown waters.

Within minutes Kuhuhu shone his light at Carter and
waved frantically. Carter churned to his side, his flippers
pumping wildly. The big man pointed to a cleat hammered
into a crack in the rock and a short length of rope attached.

Carter examined the rope. It had been cut cleanly a few
inches from the wall. The frayed end waved at them,
churned into action by the turbulence the two divers had
created.

Carter signaled for Kuhuhu to wait beside the rope. He
pointed downward and held up five fingers.

Kuhuhu nodded.

The muscular form of the AXE agent, encased in a thin
wrapper of cloth and a wet suit, eased himself forward,
using only his flippers. The downward slope continued for
twenty feet then leveled out to another opening about as
big as the first.

He found the other end of the rope. It was coiled
unevenly in a crevasse at the far end of the second flooded
cavern as if someone had tried to conceal it. One end was
frayed but the other, covered with silt, trailed off to a
corner of the large opening. It disappeared from sight at a
small opening no bigger than a man's shoulders, a man his
size, perhaps too small for a man like his companion.

The setup smelled like trouble. The rope was yellow,
usually the kind of rope left by cave explorers to lead them
back to safety. And it had been cut. If someone had
followed the rope down to the scientists and pulled the
other end back, the people he sought could still be down
there.

But how could they be down so long? Maybe they had
found a cavern large enough to sustain their interest for
days. But what about their boat? Wouldn't it still be

anchored in the lee of the island? Why would someone hide this end of the rope and leave a few inches still attached in the other cavern?

Carter had no way of answering the questions without following the rope. But he wasn't about to do it then and there. He turned to go back to Kuhuhu. They'd set up camp on the island, have something to eat, then they'd return to try and solve the mystery.

FOUR

Kuhuhu was a master at catching fish, burying them in the sand under a fire, and bringing them to a state of culinary perfection. He found root vegetables, wrapped them in leaves, and provided a feast fit for King Kamehameha.

But this was a slow process. Carter spent the time fitting the triangles of metal into a conical dish. When he'd plugged it into the transmitter and connected the fuel pack, he rotated it to find a satellite. The transmitter had a table of satellite locations shown on a decal. The closest one was directly over Oahu so he pointed the dish almost straight up and was able to code in his N3 identification to the AXE computer.

"Nicky. It's been a long time," the honeyed voice of the computer exclaimed. The joker whom Hawk had hired to bring them up to date in the world of computers had a warped sense of humor. The simulated voice sounded like a recording from some dial-a-porn number.

As usual, Carter disregarded the programmed responses and stated his business. "Patch me into Howard Schmidt," he commanded, using the push-to-talk handset attached to the transmitter.

"Where are you, Nicky?" the computer persisted while it sought the correct channel to pick up Schmidt at sea.

Carter didn't resist this time. It was sometimes useful to have the computer know exactly where he was. "You have the location where I was dropped?" he asked.

A pause. "Yes."

"We're about ten miles south at a rock outcropping that's not charted."

Schmidt's voice broke in on the exchange. "Nick? How are you, buddy?"

"Fine so far." He gave Schmidt the coordinates of the island as best he could. "We found some evidence that the expedition was sabotaged. We plan to follow it up as soon as we've had something to eat."

"We're still thirty-six hours from your location. Where will you be then? Can you send up a signal?"

"I don't know. If we're here, we will. If not, stand off and wait."

"Will do."

"What are you doing here, Howard? This isn't a matter of earth-shattering global security, you know."

"Maybe. Maybe not. I've got some gear you'll probably need."

"Like what?"

"An underwater sled, for one."

"I could get one from the navy quickly enough."

"But not one like mine," the gadget-maven said, chuckling.

Carter had his doubts about this whole assignment. The broken safety rope bothered him. But the disappearance of a ten-thousand-ton oceanography ship bothered him even more. The scenarios that whirled in his head ranged all the way from a simple change of the scientists' plans that had not been picked up on radar, to the fact that they could be dead and the ship at the bottom of the ocean.

"All right. We're going to follow the broken safety rope as far as we can. I'll try to signal you in thirty-six hours."

"This ship has to report to Pearl Harbor in forty-eight hours. We've only got maybe eight hours leeway."

"I'll do what I can," Carter replied, annoyed at the constraints. How was he to know at that moment what the caverns might contain? "I'm signing off."

"Wait a minute," Schmidt said urgently. "I should have thought of this before. Leave the earth station where it is. Turn on the red switch on the left side of the transmitter. It's a location signal. We can beam in on it."

Carter flipped the switch. "Okay?" he asked.

"Loud and clear," Schmidt replied.

The killmaster quickly considered the best location for the earth station, then moved back to the fire and his talented friend. Carter could smell the food that Kuhuhu was cooking. He hadn't realized how hungry he'd been. Kuhuhu had uncovered the fish and laid out a complete meal on broad leaves beside the fire. "What's happening?" he asked.

Carter gave him a quick rundown as he attacked his meal. He was famished. The fish was delicious and so were the root vegetables he'd never tasted before.

"I'd like to camouflage the boat," Carter announced when he'd finished eating.

"No problem," Kuhuhu said, grinning. "An old Polynesian trick." He pulled the rubber dinghy inland, his massive strength making the task seem easy. He uncovered the block and tackle from their stores, climbed a tall palm to attach a stout rope, and hauled the dinghy, supplies and all, up to the covering of dozens of palm fronds in a grove. "No one ever looks up," he explained, grinning in his own inimitable way.

Carter moved the earth station to a circle of rocks that would make it almost impossible to spot, then covered the fire pit, their tracks, and the marks left by the boat with a

broom made from dried palm fronds. "We'll skirt the
sand, then drop off a rocky shelf to get back to the cave,"
he said. "The place looks like no one has been here for
years."

Their weapons were sealed in waterproof packs strapped
close to their tanks. They tried to make silhouettes as
streamlined as possible. Carter led, falling backward into
the water. He led his friend to the cave with unerring
accuracy, holding his flashlight out in front and slightly to
one side.

In the second small cavern, the rope was still where
they'd left it. Carter hammered a climber's clamp into a
crevice and tied the yellow rope to it. He tested it for
strength and made a motion to Kuhuhu that he was going
down.

The well-muscled Kuhuhu had never admitted to a living
soul the fact that the depths of undersea caverns petrified
him. Swimming in scuba gear in shark-infested waters
held no terror for him, but the fear of the unknown and the
inky blackness of underwater research inside rock formations brought on cold sweats that could not be masked by
wet suits.

Now he followed the waving flippers of his friend through
the two caverns to a small opening. He could see from
Carter's torch that the yellow rope disappeared into the
small opening. Carter waved for him to follow and his
flippers slowly disappeared.

Kuhuhu hesitated, remembering the few times he'd agreed
to cave exploration and the times that claustrophobia had
grabbed at his gut and he'd almost panicked. Slowly and
with a dread of what was to come, the big man kicked out
with his flippers and entered the hole, his torch lighting
the sides for twenty feet ahead. Carter was already out of
sight.

The rock walls scraped at the pack on his back. Twice he was snagged on sharp outcroppings and he'd reached ahead to pull himself through, knowing a man with less strength would not have made it. Going on worried him. The return trip worried him. Everything about this job worried him.

How far had he come since entering the underground river? It seemed like forever but it had only been minutes. He brought his arms to his sides, sacrificing the light, hoping to make a slimmer profile. He pushed ahead until his massive shoulders would take him no further. He churned with his powerful legs, but he was wedged even tighter and turned slightly to face the side wall.

Back up. That was the only solution as the fear of being trapped built up in his gut. He tried to bring his arms forward to pull himself, but he couldn't move them. In the effort his hand slipped from his torch and it tumbled past his face and down the river, following the slight current.

It was dark and quiet.

Carter's light brightened as it shone through only inches of water as he shot out of the river and had to grab an outcropping beside him to avoid dropping through a dark cavern to a rock platform below. He pulled himself to a shelf of rock beside the drop-off and shone his torch down.

The small river cascaded down the side of a cavern perhaps thirty feet deep. The yellow rope followed the side of the waterfall, trailed off to the far side of the cavern, and disappeared in another hole in the rock. Carter pulled off his mouthpiece and tested the air. It was fresh. He shut off his valve to conserve air and continued his examination of the cavern.

While his flashlight was beamed on the end of the rope, Kuhuhu's torch flew out of the river and tumbled to the floor of the cavern below. At the same time, the stream of water seemed to dwindle. The torch's beam shone on one wall, illuminating the whole cavern.

Kuhuhu was in trouble. Carter figured his friend had become wedged in the tunnel and had no torch.

Carter pulled off his backpack and took out a climber's hammer and a steel chisel. With his mouthpiece back in place, he pulled his way back up the tunnel, now almost free from water. Twenty feet from the opening he found his companion, his eyes wild behind his mask, his great frame firmly wedged in the tunnel.

Carter worked frantically, small pieces of rock tumbling past him as his hammer and chisel went to work. He thought of the amount of air they had left but couldn't take the time to check his watch.

Slowly the massive shoulders started to slip through the enlarged opening. The force of the water held up behind Kuhuhu started to push him through the narrow tunnel like the cork out of a champagne bottle. But the speed they built up could be as dangerous as being wedged. If they flew out of the river to the cavern below, they could be killed outright or their bodies smashed so badly they'd never get out.

Carter wedged his flippers against the walls and signaled to Kuhuhu to take it slowly. His appeal had no effect. They moved down the small tunnel too quickly and flew out the end into the cavern.

Carter's right hand caught the yellow rope and he swung to one side as they popped out. With his left he tried to catch Kuhuhu, but the big man's wet suit was too slippery. The killmaster watched helplessly as Stonewall Kuhuhu flew past him and landed in a heap far below, Carter's torch beside him pointing at a pool that was beginning to form under the big man. It looked like blood, but Carter couldn't tell at that distance.

Carter swung down the rope hand-over-hand. He'd misjudged the distance in the faint light. It was more like a hundred feet to the rock below. He reached the massive form in seconds but time made no difference now. The side of Kuhuhu's head was crushed and while Carter watched, the valiant heart stopped pumping blood from the crushed skull.

The bloody mouthpiece dangled on its hose beside his mouth. Carter shut off the valve on his gear and shut off the one that Kuhuhu no longer needed.

Carter looked at the bulk of his friend and decided to strip him of his burdens. He took off the backpack and put it to one side. The scuba gear he stuffed in a deep crevice in a dark corner of the cavern. He pulled the big man to one side of the cavern and covered his body with rocks that were strewn around the cave. Carter stood motionless over his friend's tomb for a few moments, thinking of some of the good times they'd shared in the past.

He was in no hurry. He had all the time in the world to mourn his friend. He figured the scientists were either dead or safe in some other cavern.

Carter had only one course of action that made sense. He crawled to the end of the yellow rope and examined the opening where it disappeared again. He took a last look at Kuhuhu's tomb, washed his mouthpiece in the nearby waterfall, and put it in his mouth. With one flashlight in his right hand and the other tucked in his belt, he started down the second river.

Who would be there to take him out should he become wedged as Kuhuhu had earlier? What was at the end of the river? How far down was he and how far did he have to go? He cursed his luck at losing his old friend as a torrent of questions flooded his brain. He'd lost too many partners through the years, but never one to such a stupid accident.

This river was steeper but wider. As far as he could tell, he'd traveled about a hundred and fifty feet before he came out at a water-filled cavern that gave him more freedom to explore.

Nothing of interest could be found in the undersea cavern except the yellow rope that wound its way inexorably downward into another narrow opening. This time, the water cascaded down a hole about ten feet wide and the rope continued across the few feet to a dry tunnel.

The physics of undersea caves was a mystery to Carter. How could some of the caverns so far below the level of the sea escape flooding? Why was he now in a dry tunnel that still led downward? Maybe the water had been diverted in another direction. Such diversions were the only explanations he could come up with. The cavern where Kuhuhu was lying under a pile of rock had escaped filling because the outflow was at least equal to the inflow. But where had the fresh air come from?

The dry tunnel led downward, sometimes leveling off only to turn downward again. He figured he was about five hundred feet below the sea and still the rope continued to draw him forward.

He came out at a partially water-filled cavern, this one much smaller. The water flowed out through another tunnel while the yellow rope snaked through a dry tunnel ten feet above the level of the water.

Carter tried to pull himself up by the rope, but it was loose at the other end. He had to climb the sheer rock face using his own rope and steel climbers' cleats. At the top he entered the dry tunnel and followed the rope for fifty feet where it ended in a neat coil.

The tunnel continued straight ahead. He shone his torch but could see only rock walls in a tunnel about six feet in diameter.

He had to go on. The tunnel led to another cavern, this one filled almost to the top by water. He rested for a few minutes to conserve the precious air in his tank, then explored the undersea lake for an exit.

He found one at the other side and about twenty feet down. Again, after about twenty feet, the water dropped away in an underground waterfall, leaving him in a tunnel that was dry and dark.

He tested the air. It was foul. Quickly he used his breathing apparatus and searched his weary brain for the familiar smell that fouled the air. It really wasn't difficult. He'd smelled the stench of decomposing bodies often enough.

The tunnel came out at a ledge down on another small lake. He shone his torch around. The body of a man, or what remained of it, was wedged against a back wall, a harpoon sticking from his chest. Ocean crab swarmed over the remains, slowly devouring it. He turned away with a shudder.

Carter swung his light around the rest of the shelf and found nothing. He shone the light on the surface of the lake and found two bloated bodies half submerged in the water, encrusted with scores of voracious crabs.

He'd found his scientists, and the assignment suddenly took on a whole new dimension. Someone had killed them, someone who must have had a compelling reason, someone who probably had something to hide.

Carter searched the water thoroughly and found one other body. The weight of its equipment was too heavy for the amount of buoyant flesh remaining. He could still tell that it was a man. The tally was four men, all with harpoons sticking from half-eaten flesh.

But where was the woman?

The only way was down. He checked his watch. With

fresh air in dry caverns and walkways, he'd only used half of his full hour of air. But half meant he was not about to get back to the surface using his own tank. He could hold his breath for part of the time and Schmidt's scuba tube would give him another ten minutes, but that wouldn't be nearly enough, not if he went on.

The polluted lake led him to another underground river, this one wider, the current faster. Water tugged at him and pulled him on as the drop became steeper.

He felt like a roach being pulled down an open sink drain, a swirling vortex that became more of a whirlpool as he reached the bottom.

Suddenly he was in free fall, clawing at unresisting air, thinking of the fate that had befallen his friend Stonewall Kuhuhu.

He didn't have time to think it through before falling into another body of water. His mind played tricks on him. Perhaps it was the compressed air he'd been breathing. While falling, and before hitting the surface of another lake, he thought he'd seen what appeared to be a fairyland of color with people dressed in formal evening clothes walking beside the lake.

Carter surfaced at the base of a monstrous fountain that spewed water to a height of fifty feet. He swam to the side of the lake and found himself staring up at scores of curious faces, all looking down at him and smiling.

FIVE

The people ranged in age from about twenty to fifty and they all had one thing in common: they were as perfect as possible, wrinkle-free, happy and smiling. The formal clothes Carter thought had been an hallucination were real. The women wore a variety of styles, long and short, bright and dark, some enhanced with precious gems set in filigreed silver or gold. The men were in black tie, white tie, some in military dress uniforms. All were impeccable and handsome.

Four men, none less than six feet six inches tall, parted the crowd with care and pulled Carter from the water. They stripped him to his wet undergarments, confiscating his Luger and stiletto, and led him away, accompanied by the cooing of admiring females.

Carter was left unguarded in a luxury bedroom that rivaled those of Bangkok's Oriental Hotel, rated the best in the world for the past few years. A dresser was filled with underclothes of all sizes. The closets were filled with clothes of every kind, arranged into work clothes, casual, and formal.

The man from AXE decided he might as well go with the flow. He searched the bathroom for listening devices and made sure the mirror wasn't one-way glass before he stripped off the tiny gas bomb and Schmidt's scuba device. He showered in the huge bathroom of pink marble, replaced his equipment with the old tape, and donned the boxer shorts he'd carried with him to the bathroom.

Carter finished dressing in the bedroom and soon stood in front of a full-length mirror in black tie. While dressing, he wondered how they managed to bring in the material, the marble, the clothes, the furniture. They had to have an access port big enough to allow a submarine to enter, one large enough to transport almost anything.

The guards must have had a camera concealed in the bedroom and observed his dressing. As soon as his tie was straight and his hair combed, they came for him, the same four men, in the same military-cut uniforms, all four exactly alike in form and feature, as alike as peas in a pod.

Am I dreaming? Carter wondered.

He was led from room to room, past hundreds of beautiful people in dinner clothes, through massive lounges, and finally into an intimate apartment that made the room he'd been given seem like a hovel. The walls were glazed by something that looked like a glossy silicone. It gave off its own light. The furniture was soft and inviting. On a raised dais, a man sat alone, smiling down at him.

He was a man of average height, not abnormal in any way—at first glance. On closer inspection his eyes were like deep pools of mercury, hypnotic, compelling—eyes that once seen would never be forgotten. And his features were perfect, unlined, his teeth capped, his hair full and glossy. He beckoned Carter to sit beside him in a similar chair, similar but at a level two feet lower. When they'd been served a steaming brew that tasted like coffee laced with a liqueur, he spoke for the first time. His voice sounded like a recording, the bass notes attenuated abnormally.

"First we'll find out who you are. Look straight ahead, please," the voice said, its tone like a drug, commanding without force or threat.

Carter complied. A screen in front of them came to life with thousands of faces flashing past at the rate of hundreds a second. Suddenly Carter was looking at his own face. It stayed on the screen for a moment before it faded and a history followed:

Nicholas Carter. Age unknown but assumed to be late thirties to early forties, six feet one in height, dark brown eyes and hair, multiple scars on body. Carter is the most highly rated agent of AXE, an ultrasecret intelligence agency known to only a few people. Carter is designated N3, Killmaster, authorized to kill in the line of duty.

The screen showed nothing for a few moments and then continued:

AXE, fronted by Amalgamated Press and Wire Services located on Dupont Circle in Washington, is headed by one David Hawk, confidant of the president of the United States and selected members of his cabinet. Hawk, thought to be the best man at his job in the West, started with Donovan as a teen-ager in the OSS in WW II.

The account went on to give Hawk's description, and full details on the appearance and responsibilities of Ginger Bateman, Rupert Smith, and Howard Schmidt. It ended with one comment:

On success of mission, recommend elimination of all AXE personnel, high priority.

"You seem to have the better of me," Carter said, selecting a cigarette from an ornate silver box on the table beside him and lighting it with a matching lighter.

"Xanax Zendal," the voice said. "This is my main base. You will be comfortable here, temporarily."

"I wasn't thrilled with the last statement on your screen," Carter said as casually as he was able.

"Nothing personal, Mr. Carter. All intelligence agencies must be eliminated eventually. It would seem prudent to eliminate the best one first."

"If you are to meet your objectives," Carter finished for him.

"Exactly. How refreshing to speak with an outsider who understands."

Carter sighed, dragged on his cigarette, and thought about the number of men he'd encountered like this one. The thought was momentary. It was one of several that took only microseconds and didn't divert his attention from the man before him. What would the average Joe, the man on the street think if he knew of all the crackpots who were trying to become demigods and eventually take over the world? Carter didn't have to have the scenario spelled out for him, but to formulate a plan of his own he would have to learn all he could about this one. How extensive was his organization? When did he plan to make his first major strike? What was his ultimate objective? How was he supplied and where did the underwater ship enter their kingdom? The place appeared to be quite extensive.

One thing, however, was common to all the men like Zendal he'd ever met: they were proud of their accomplishments and could easily rationalize their position. They were usually not averse to boasting about their plans.

"The walls," he began. "They seem to be fluorescent."

"A spray process that one of my people invented. I was thinking of a glass dome, but he convinced me we'd be less detectable if we pulverized millions of tons of sandstone, vacuumed out the powder, and sprayed the walls with his new silicone fluorescent. We're surrounded by volcanic rock, the best support we could possibly find."

"It seems extensive."

"You've only seen a fraction of the caverns," Zendal

said. "They go on for more than a mile." He waved a hand at one of the tall guards who carried a tray of beverages. "We drink only fruit juices here, Carter. What would you like?"

"I'll pass. Fruit juice has never been one of my vices."

"Decadence. That's what . . ." Zendal started to say, his face suffused with blood for a moment before he regained control. In those few seconds Carter was reminded of old newsreels he'd seen of Hitler when he was annoyed.

"Something about the people," Carter took another tack. "They all look so happy, so healthy. They seem to be in a festive mood."

"Every man and woman in the world, your world, wants to be attractive and healthy. Your society cannot guarantee that. I can."

"Zendal's fountain of youth?" Carter asked, trying to keep mockery out of his tone. Where did he get that name? he mused. Some kid's sci-fi comic?

The man was beyond absorbing sarcasm. Madmen seldom recognized criticism unless it was overt. "Plastic surgery," he answered. "The best dentistry, a complete transplant program. No one need suffer or feel old. No one need feel lonesome or unappreciated."

"So you've cured every ailment known to mankind?"

"Not yet," the giant ego responded as if the problem were not out of his reach. "Selection, Carter. You find a genius suffering from a kidney ailment, hounded by a harpy of a wife, unappreciated by an indifferent government," the man said, looking down at Carter, sipping at an orange-colored drink. "My agents approach him, convince him he is worthy of a better life. It's seldom a scientist is so nationalistic that he puts patriotism before his own comfort."

"And your agents have been processed. They are like the beautiful people I saw earlier."

"You learn quickly, Carter. Women recruit men. Men recruit women. Sometimes, not often, we find a mind so brilliant we break a rule and send a man after a man."

"Decent of you," Carter said. "You're sure you don't have a scotch and soda somewhere, a gin and tonic, perhaps a brandy?"

Self-deluded monsters of Zendal's caliber didn't react to subtle jabs at their philosophies, but they reacted violently to direct attacks. Carter had dealt with the breed before. His intention was to keep the man off guard without going too far. His usual ploy was to prod them into boasting of their accomplishments and showing more than was prudent. He usually succeeded. No matter how brilliant the mind, the breed was driven by vanity and that conceit was their Achilles' heel in the end.

"You must have a complicated source of supply to keep your population fed and clothed," Carter commented lightly.

"Not too complicated, really. The seas are vast, Carter. I have transport submarines and supply ships. There are hundreds of uncharted coves in these waters for off-loading. The best radar in the world cannot cover the globe."

"I'd like to see the submarine pens."

"And you shall," he said, turning in his seat to face Carter. "You have two options. You will join us or you will die. Either way, I'd be pleased to show you my whole operation."

The look on his face as he made the pronouncement was classic. Hitler had the look. If history could have recorded it, Stalin, Genghis Khan, Alexander the Great—all the conquerors who had the same kind of inflated ego would have had the look. It was a kind of madness, an unwillingness to recognize the rules of society, any outside society, any rules that were not their own.

"Like the scientists I found on the way in?"

"Unfortunate. What a waste. Flaws in our clones, I'm afraid. They reacted too quickly. The problem's already been corrected."

"The waiter?" Carter asked. "A clone like the others?"

"Any productive society needs service. But slavery breeds discontent. The simple solution is either cloning or robotry. We're further advanced in cloning at present. Mine have some electronic assistance—bionic clones you might say."

"Subhumans."

"Not even that, Carter. Synthetic flesh, some electronics, some human cells used to cover the innards and make them appear human."

"What about funding? You can't sit down here and print your own money," Carter said, realizing he might just have spoken the truth.

"Old-fashioned. Sloppy. Too much room for error. No, Mr. Carter, we use more sophisticated means," Zendal said, a satisfied smile on his handsome face. "I have the best computer minds in existence. Taking money from the banks and depositing it in my accounts is child's play for them. It's become a game, like the way an average family might play a board game on a rainy day. We follow the progress of all nations and use the transfers as a form of punishment. Of course, they don't know where the money went or why. We have to be satisfied in our own minds that we have played the game well."

The man's worse than I thought, Carter told himself. The sooner he got out, the better. He'd radio Schmidt and make sure the government used the military to take care of this crackpot. But how would he convince them of the truth? It sounded like a nightmare, not a rational explanation for the deaths of a handful of scientists.

First he had to find out how this madman was going to

take over the world or whatever was on his warped agenda. "Your computer screen showed that you plan to wipe out my organization. Why mine?" he asked.

"You perhaps weren't listening. I said I'd have to eliminate *all* intelligence agencies."

"Then the politicians, then all military officers, then the teachers," Carter finished for him.

"Not necessarily in that order. But yes, they have to go."

"So you can build a new society, a better society," he said, not hiding his sarcasm this time. "Why does it always sound the same in the end? You know better, right? You won't make the same mistakes, right? It takes one hell of an ego to think he can rule the world without making the same mistakes as other mortal men."

"Come, Mr. Carter. I see you have to be convinced," Zendal said, rising from his chair and guiding Carter toward a massive door in his chamber.

They climbed aboard a two-man car and were whisked away from Zendal's apartment at high speed. In minutes Zendal used a special plastic card to open a pair of steel doors. They entered and were looking up at a mass of tubes and wires circling a tubular structure that appeared to rise to the roof of the cavern.

"Nothing extraordinary about this, Carter. An oversize laser. With it I can cut through three-inch steel twenty miles away."

"Impressive."

"The next chamber is even more impressive but you shall not see it. Not unless you decide to join us."

"Magnetic rays. Science-fiction stuff, I suppose," Carter mocked.

"How could you know? Who could have told you?" Zendal asked, almost in a rage.

"I suppose you have massive jamming devices that screw up compass readings and make radio contact useless," he prodded further.

Zendal controlled himself and said nothing. But in this case, his silence was pregnant with possibilities. The crazy ideas Carter had thrown out were close to the truth. Lasers, magnetic fields of force, jamming devices. It seemed reasonable considering all the talent the man had coerced into coming here.

Since Zendal wasn't responding, Carter decided that silence was also the best course. He'd been joking and obviously hit a nerve. "Where are the submarine pens?" he finally asked.

"Next stop on the tour," Zendal boasted, the incident already forgotten.

Again, Carter couldn't help but compare this man with others like him through the years. The man's brain seemed to be compartmentalized. He wasn't limited only to tunnel vision, he had tunnel senses. He didn't hear suggestions that didn't fit his plans. If he did allow a foreign thought to penetrate, his brain rejected it out of hand.

The car sped along the narrow road at about thirty miles an hour and it seemed like twice the speed in the narrow corridors. Carter memorized every twist and turn on the route and knew how long it took to get from one place to another. An overall plan of the underground city was forming in his mind.

Without warning, they rounded a corner and were dwarfed by two submarines tied up at cement piers, both being unloaded. The cargo included people who were strapped to stretchers and appeared to be unconscious.

"Donors," Zendal volunteered. "Not easy to find. They have to be indigents who are relatively healthy and completely unattached. Tissue matching is very difficult on the mainland. One has to have a complete organization."

He said it as if the butcher shops he was running were a minor annoyance and the unwilling donors ungrateful. Carter was learning more than he'd bargained for, but he still didn't know the major moves Zendal planned.

"Fixed laser beams and magnetic fields that have limited range won't blackmail the world into submission. What are you going to do, build a nuclear bomb?" he asked.

"Very good, Mr. Carter. Full marks. I have the people who can do it. I can steal the plutonium. But I don't want to go through the motions. Too slow. And I'd end up with a second- or third-generation device instead of the best."

"What then?"

"Steal what I want. Your navy is sending out a new destroyer for field trials. They are overconfident fat cats who think the small ship is invincible."

"You can't steal it and run it with your own people. The navy'll send out the whole fleet if necessary and blow you out of the water."

"I don't want the ship, Carter. I want the six nuclear devices it carries."

"How . . . ?"

"Intelligence. You saw my identification file and the data we have on you. I've got people in the Pentagon, the State Department, the White House."

"But the new ship's orders will be sealed. Not even Admiral Brenner has been given a copy."

"I saw the orders before they were sealed and delivered. The ship will pass within ten miles of this base. I can draw the ship off course to within range, then use my lasers to open it like a can of peas at the waterline. It'll go down like a stone," Zendal boasted, his face a broad grin. "My clones will be waiting for it at two hundred fathoms. I have launching chambers here and on one other island."

While they rode back to the main dining room, Carter's mind was going over all the possibilities. He'd seen his wet suit and backpack in a guardhouse not far from the submarine pens. He had to get out and tell Schmidt so he'd be able to alert the navy.

But would they believe him? The military had a natural suspicion of information not from their own brass. They also had their share of large egos. And what had happened to the woman scientist in the group he'd come to save? Were they conditioning her now? Would she end up as one of them, coiffed, manicured, tummy-tucked, and with a mouthful of teeth the envy of Farah Fawcett?

And what of the hundreds of people, perhaps thousands, who were there now? If the navy believed his story, they'd blast these caverns to dust. And if they didn't believe him and he had to stop this madman himself, how was he going to get the disillusioned innocents out? And once out, would they fit back into the world above?

The answers his reeling brain supplied were disquieting. He couldn't let the navy or any other force destroy thousands just because they'd been deluded by a megalomaniac. Somehow these brainwashed souls could be made productive members of society. So in the long run it was going to be up to him. He'd warn the navy to protect their ship, but that was as far as he was going to go.

While his mind was at work, they arrived at a dining room that looked like first class on the *Queen Elizabeth 2*. The tables were filled with beautiful people chatting and laughing. A string quartet played a Beethoven sonata. Waiters carried trays of food that smelled like dishes from the kitchens of Lutèce and Le Cygne in New York. The clones apparently could be taught both basic and artful skills. They lacked the will to change or better themselves. They existed solely to serve their masters. It was truly a controlled, twentieth-century form of slavery.

Carter looked around at the other diners. He almost doubted if these people could ever be brought back to the real world, or that they would leave of their own free will. But he couldn't destroy them with the installation. It was one hell of a problem.

During the first course, while Zendal was in an expansive mood, Carter asked the final question, the final piece of his jigsaw. "The men in the cavern who were killed by your guards—did any survive?"

"Survive? Unfortunately, no. I understand one was a Ph.D. in oceanography and had a masters in archaeology. Or was it the other way around?"

"It's strange that they had only one scientist in the group," Carter commented.

"They had a woman, a Ph.D. in anthropology. She must have gone down with the ship. Unfortunate waste. We could have used them both."

Gone down with the ship. Carter's jaw tightened. So they had sunk the *Sir Wilfred Laurier*. It was lying on the bottom somewhere near the island. The bastard! He was totally cold-blooded.

And the woman—what was her name? Dr. Barbara Wall—must have gone down with the ship. There was no way they'd have kept her from the descent unless she'd been ill. Perhaps that was it; she'd been ill and stayed on board. It didn't matter now. She was just as dead one way as the other.

He looked around the room while he poked without appetite at his steak tartare. Everyone looked so damned happy. Was it all one great charade, or were they fed . . . ?

He put down his fork and looked at his plate. He'd only had one mouthful of the meat. Better leave the rest, he thought. Zendal might have brought them all to the caverns willingly, but he might be keeping them in a state of euphoria with drugs in their food and drink. Perhaps that was the reason for the ban on alcohol. A drugged population couldn't tolerate liquor of any kind.

Carter played with his food, not eating any while he looked around the room. They were under guard. Some of the clones stood at the entrances with strange-looking automatic weapons. He knew where he'd seen something like them. Schmidt had shown him the latest in caseless ammunition. These submachine guns could spit out a thousand rounds a minute with no appreciable recoil. The projectiles had no casings, so the square magazines that made up most of their bulk held hundreds of rounds instead of the usual twenty or thirty of more conventional weapons.

"The men's room?" Carter whispered to his host.

"No problem." Zendal clapped his hands and four waiters put down their trays to surround Carter and escort him away. His last glimpse of the dining room showed more than five hundred people, all in excited conversation, enjoying their meal, totally unaware of the stranger who was under guard. It wasn't natural. But then, nothing in this place was.

SIX

Carter felt like an army miscreant being marched to face his CO, but this was much more unusual. The four guards towered over him by several inches, they all looked alike, their pace was identical, and they all seemed to think the same, if they actually thought at all.

Near the men's room outside the dining area, one of the armed guards joined them. The six marched into the white-tiled rest room to find several men in the process of relieving themselves.

"You will clear this area," one of the clones said while Carter closed himself in an empty booth.

The noise in the room decreased to almost nothing, just the breathing of the five guards. Obviously the other men had all cleared out. Carter sat on the seat, his pants and boxer shorts around his ankles, his right hand busily peeling the tape away from Pierre. While he was in the process, he peeled off the small scuba device, placed it in his right-hand jacket pocket, and thanked his lucky stars that they'd missed these two items when they'd first found him. He could understand their not finding Pierre, but not noticing the scuba tube's bulge under his long johns was a fortunate oversight.

The time was right. He zipped his pants, flushed the toilet, and walked out, the small bomb in his hand. He took a deep breath, twisted the two halves of the bomb, and dropped it on the floor in the middle of the five startled guards.

They did appear to be capable of emotion. The surprise changed to fear, but they didn't inhale. Something in their makeup—flesh, plastic or electronic—told them to imitate the prisoner's action.

Carter didn't wait for them to take the initiative. He drove his fist into the guard holding the submachine gun and snatched the weapon from him as the clone gulped in lethal gas and crumbled.

The others moved in. Carter gut-punched two in lightning succession using the butt of the gun, then whipped around, using his right heel in a judo move on the other two.

It was a scene familiar to the Killmaster. One blow usually forced the enemy to take a breath and Pierre did the rest. He was the only one left standing. It took him less than two minutes to change into one of the guard's clothes and make his way outside and find one of the two-man transport cars.

Armed with the lethal modern machine gun, he headed for the guardhouse where he'd seen his wet suit and backpack. No one stopped him. While sitting at the controls, the too-large uniform wasn't obvious. It wasn't until he arrived at the guardhouse that it was easy to see that he was not one of them.

Two guards were on duty. They raised their weapons but each took three rounds of the caseless ammunition in the chest before they could react fully. They backed up against the wall, then slid to the floor leaving ugly red streams running slowly downward.

Carter dragged them into the guardroom and looked outside to see if the firing had drawn attention. It was an almost deserted part of the vast cavern. No one was in sight. He pulled on the dry underclothes he'd worn with the wet suit and forced the tight-fitting rubber suit over it. The guard's uniform went on over the black rubber for camouflage. He checked his pack and found it had been untouched.

The corridor was still deserted and the transporter was still outside. No alarm had been raised as far as he knew. It was about five minutes since he'd left the men's room. Zendal had to be aware that his security had been breached.

The corridor to the sub pens passed the quarters of the clones, dormitories lined with bunks in the military fashion. One was for female clones.

He saw more activity as he neared the sub pens. Clones and men in white lab coats fussed around the two subs that were still unloading. He parked the transporter and walked confidently to a scientist who was working alone at a control board. He shoved the machine gun barrel at the man's chest. "How do I enter the air lock?" he asked.

"Who the hell are you? You're not a guard . . ." He was about to sound an alarm when Carter shoved the barrel into the man's diaphragm, making him wince with pain.

"Don't be a fool. You don't want to die now," he hissed. "Show me how to get out of here."

The white-coated man led the way in a daze. No one paid any attention to them. He led the way to an air lock and on Carter's order closed the door after them.

"Fill the chamber with water and open the outer door," Carter commanded when they were secure and out of sight.

"But I'll drown," the man said, his voice a mere squeak as his fear took over.

"You've got one chance," Carter said. "I'll get out as fast as I can. Hold your breath and close the outer chamber as soon as I'm out."

"But I can't!"

"Then you'll die. Get moving!" Carter shouted at him as he heard the general alarm, like the wail of a siren, muffled by the airtight room.

The sound of compressed air or released hydraulics sounded as the scientist turned a valve. One side of the room started to open to the sea and water rushed in at their feet. Carter prepared to leave, using the gun's sling to shoulder the weapon and free both his hands.

"I'll drown!" the man cried as Carter attempted to pull himself through against the strong inflow of water. The last thing he saw was the man standing up to his waist in the surge of dark water.

The sea was black and the pressure more than he'd experienced without scuba equipment. The largest cavern had to be two hundred feet from top to bottom and he'd worked his way several hundred feet down to get there. If he tried to find the surface too fast, he'd get the bends. If he moved too slowly, they would be waiting for him on the surface.

Through years of yoga training, he had the ability to hold his breath for four minutes, more if he pressed it. Better call that three minutes under this kind of pressure. The small scuba device would give him another ten minutes according to Schmidt.

He moved his hands, fanning the water, making sure he didn't rise too fast. It was still totally black. He had no idea whether it was night or day, whether the sun would eventually lighten the water near the surface or he'd break the surface in darkness. Given the choice he'd opt for darkness, but that meant he still didn't know how far down he was.

Three minutes must have passed as Carter's lungs began to scream for air. He pulled the plastic mouthpiece from the small tube, clamped it between his teeth, and applied pressure.

Compressed oxygen flowed into his mouth at a rate determined by how hard he bit down on the plastic. He'd have preferred some practice with the gadget, but the time for that was past. He had to breathe through his mouth and blow out through his nose. It took him at least half a minute to adjust to the rhythm.

The pressure of the sea was no longer crushing against him as it had when he exited the sub pen. It had to be ten minutes now and he was still not at the surface. He couldn't have more than three minutes of air left and he felt the beginning of the bends attack his gut.

He'd come up too fast. The bubbles of nitrogen in his bloodstream might not be extensive but what he had were painful. He'd had no choice. It was either a mild case of the bends or death by drowning.

Though he knew he was close to the surface, he also realized he wasn't out of danger. He could hear the propellers of small search boats, could see them churn the water above him. He waited for a period of relative calm and poked his head above water, letting the scuba tube sink to the bottom as he drew in a welcome lungful of fresh air.

He counted six boats in the distance. It seemed they were fanning out to sea. They must have searched the island first, then the shore close in.

The moon was full but was hidden behind clouds, making the sea and the island dark and forbidding. Carter swam to the beach and crept out, keeping to the dark outline of rock until he was onshore. The sand had been churned up by searchers but the island seemed deserted. He opened one of the packs and armed himself. With the packs hidden and one of the enemy's guns cocked and ready, he made a quick sweep search, the submachine gun held in front of him. He didn't want to be vulnerable while he hauled the rubber dinghy down.

The dinghy and his equipment would be heavy for one man to lower, but he wrapped the rope around the twisted bowl of a coconut palm, released the block and tackle, and sat, his feet against the palm trunk as he let the rope feed around the trunk slowly.

Carter's supplies were all there. He added the packs he'd salvaged, then hauled the boat to the shore and into the mild surf. He knew there was no way he could stay on this island; anywhere was safer than here. He took one minute to fill his tanks from the bobbing fake albatross, then hauled on the gear shift and accelerator levers at the same time. The twin Johnsons roared and churned the inky water at full revs. He'd made it. He'd stop at a nearby island, call Schmidt on the land station, and wait for reinforcements.

The moon had come out from behind a cloud. Carter was able to sea the shape of the horizon for the first time. One peak rose above the others in the distance and he headed for it, locking the common tiller for the twin motors and taking stock of what was on board. He wasn't about to unpack his own weapons. They'd been with him too long to be soaked in saltwater. He examined the submachine gun he's captured. The unusual design kept the rectangular ammunition box waterproof. He cocked the gun, putting one round in the chamber. Water could have entered the barrel and the trigger mechanism. But Carter wasn't concerned about the long-term effect of the brine. The weapon would perform for as long as he needed it.

He opened some of the packs. One contained the earth station, another was filled with emergency cooking gear and supplies. Good. He'd be able to have a meal when he hit dry land.

It was too soon to feel secure. He was entering the perimeter of the boats that had fanned out looking for him. They spotted the lone rubber dinghy among all the steel hulls and the chase was on.

Carter knew he couldn't outrun them, his seventy-five Johnsons against their jet motors. So he plowed on, cocked the weapon, and waited for them to come within range.

At first it was like shooting the proverbial fish in a rain barrel. They seemed to come on without regard for his firepower. He stripped three boats of their passengers and left them careening wildly out to sea before one of them tried a kamikaze move, heading straight for him, all guns blazing, and running him over as steel-jacketed slugs tore at the hard rubber of his craft.

The tactic was too much for the smaller craft. Even without being run over by the steel hull, the holes from the 7.62mm slugs would have sunk her.

Carter was underwater again. He churned from left to right looking for the packs he'd lost and found then slowly sinking into the black depths. He was able to round them up and hold their straps over one arm while treading water. The weight of the waterproof packs and his efforts neutralized each other at about twenty feet underwater.

Again he waited, holding his breath, watching the sea churn around him as the jets and a few propellers cut through the water over his head.

It seemed an eternity until all was quiet above. Carter had been counting off the seconds. He got to about two hundred when he decided it was safe to surface. He pulled the plug on the flotation chambers of his packs and bobbed to the surface as they filled with compressed air.

The remains of the small fleet were about a half mile away, heading for their home base. The peak Carter had selected as his target was about five miles away, probably ten miles from Zendal's unnatural kingdom.

Carter took straps from two or three packs in each hand and started to churn with his feet in a powerful butterfly kick. He couldn't keep his head raised all the time, so he raised it every few seconds to keep his direction and plowed on.

Five miles was not a real challenge for the Killmaster. He'd done twenty miles more than once, but he still suffered from a mild case of the bends and the sea battle had been a drain on his energy. When he finally circled the towering rock and found a small secluded beach, he was almost exhausted.

Carter dragged his supplies to the shadows of a clump of squat pineapple palm and lay back on the sand to gain his strength. The bends had almost disappeared, but he was cold and hungry. He took off his wet suit and the cotton long johns he wore beneath it and hung them on clumps of palmetto to dry. The night was not cold now that he was out of the wet suit. A balmy Pacific breeze caressed his skin. It was mild and warm.

Carter's first priority was communication. He assembled the land station and pointed it toward the sky over Hawaii. It needed little adjustment to come to full power.

He pressed the talk button and sent out the recognition signal, "N3 calling HS." He repeated the call three times before Schmidt came back.

"Schmidt. We're still twelve hours out. Are you still at the same location?"

"Negative. I'm about ten miles south. You've got to find a way to get to me without causing suspicion."

"Say again. Suspicion from whom?"

"This is going to sound crazy. You'll believe it because you know me. But no one else will."

"Try me."

"We've got a mad scientist on our hands. This is comic-book stuff. But the guy's for real."

"Dangerous?"

"Affirmative. He's enticed a choice crowd of scientists to join him. They've developed powerful magnetic fields and the biggest laser beam I've ever seen. They can do a lot of damage."

"Not from there they can't," Schmidt offered.

"Don't bet on it. The navy's sending a new destroyer out for sea trials—the newest weapon they've got. This madman, name's Zendal, knows the ship's going to pass by his island. He plans to bring the ship close to him by magnetic force and use the laser to open her up like a can of corn."

"Why sink her? Why not just take her?" Schmidt asked.

"He'll try, but give the navy credit. They won't give up without a fight. He'll split her open, sink her in about seventy fathoms, and steal the six nuclear missiles on board."

"So what else is new? Every crazed gang of fanatics is trying for nuclear thefts now. I heard the Palestinians got their hands on one last week."

Carter didn't want to go into all the details, but he had to give Schmidt at least the minimum. "Here's the rest of it. He's got close to a thousand people down there with him—a kind of underwater kingdom. They act far too cheerful—it's as if they've been drugged. I'm sure he got them there with legitimate incentives, but he's keeping them in a pink cloud now so they won't change their minds. We've got to free them before we can destroy him.''

"So let the navy do it."

"I don't see how we can. It would be war any way they played it. Most of the innocents would be killed.''

"Speaking of innocents, what happened to the people you went after?''

"Dead. This Zendal's got an army of—get this—clones. They killed the Canadians and sank the research vessel. But I've got a feeling the woman scientist is alive. I've got a gut feeling he's holding her, maybe going to try to convert her because her knowledge of oceanography would be a great help to him.

"What do you think you can do?"

"I don't know. But I need transportation. For once I'd be happy to see all the gadgets you can pull out of your hat.''

"How'd the scuba tube work?''

"Like a charm. I'll tell you about it one day but not now. I need transport and I need weapons.''

"You've got both. Any idea what's the best way to get to you undetected?''

"Are you close to any of the trade routes?'' Carter asked.

He could hear Schmidt confer with the captain. "Captain says we're only ten miles from one of the Hawaii-Tahiti runs.''

"Okay. Track the run so Zendal will think you're friendly. Can you spring my transport yourself?''

"No problem.''

"We'll need some unique camouflage.''

"I've thought of that.''

"You've got to warn Admiral Brenner. I can predict his reaction, but we've got to tell him anyway."

"We could need him later to pick up the innocents you talked about. How do you plan to get them to safety?"

"I'll take care of that. Just notify Brenner and let it take its course. If I know the military mind, he'll think we're crazy and issue no special orders."

"That's it? Can I reach you there anytime?"

"I'm not going anywhere, Howard, old boy. Just get me the damned boat, or whatever it is, as fast as you can."

Zendal sat in his throne room with his security chiefs around him. "Are we certain the man Carter is dead? He knows too much to live."

They weren't about to remind him that Carter's knowledge was his fault. It was part of the ego problem they had to deal with every day. "He's dead. We saw him go down with his boat."

"Remember that he survived an escape from one of our chambers. How do you explain that?"

"We can't, Excellency. But one of my best men was in one of the boats. We don't have to rely on the word of clones. Carter is dead."

"How long did you circle the downed craft?" Zendal asked. Carter had fooled him before. He couldn't afford to take any chances. He had too much at stake.

"Five minutes, Excellency. No man could have lived through our attack."

"Very well. I've been informed that our target has left Pearl Harbor," Zendal announced, his unusual mercury-colored eyes aflame with excitement. "When it reaches its closest point to us, we will commence our project."

They stood to leave.

"You will not rise in my presence," Zendal screamed at them.

They all sat and waited for him to rise and leave. Then they left in twos and threes, every man grumbling at the humility of catering to the man's ego. They were trapped as much as the others, the ones he fed and clothed regally. They hated him, but they were not going to back away now. If it weren't for all the money he promised. . . .

SEVEN

The first order of business finished, Carter searched for dry brush firewood. He soon had a fire going and a pan of saltwater bass and some fries sizzling in a thin coating of vegetable oil. The fish had come from the sea after ten minutes of patient wading with a sharp stick poised in his right hand. The potatoes and oil had been in one of the packs.

The smell of the cooking food made his mouth water. When he was able to dish up the food in an army-issue mess can, it was the best he'd tasted in as long as he could remember.

Carter scoured his cooking gear with beach sand and stowed everything in the packs, everything but the land station. He placed that on a flat rock near the sand where it was out of the way but within easy reach.

The sand was warm under his back. The sky had cleared and was studded with jewels that flashed down at Carter like those in photos in travel brochures back home. Things weren't all that bad. He'd had one hell of a day but here he was on a Pacific island, the balmy breezes caressing his skin, plenty of fish in the sea, and his old buddy Schmidt on his way to provision him. The death of Stonewall Kuhuhu saddened him, however.

He was about to take out his personal weapons and check them when something sprang at him from out of the darkness. It was smaller than he was, with long hair and sharp talons. It knocked the wind out of Carter in its first charge as it came through the air, landing on his belly with all its weight.

Carter was on his feet in a split second, gasping for air, but his attacker was faster. Before Carter could get set, a judo chop caught him in his unprotected belly and a swinging reverse leg kick caught him on the side of the head. He went down, grazing his head against a rock. A red haze blocked his vision as he took two more kicks to the ribs that almost broke the bones.

His confused mind dreamed up all kind of horror stories while he was trying to orient himself. Was it one of the shell-shocked Japanese who had held out after the war? Were aboriginal tribes still inhabiting these deserted rocks? He was coherent enough to erase the last assumption. The attack had come from an expert in the martial arts.

His assailant was violent in its attack, panting and grunting with fear and effort. With Carter down, it flew at him before he could recover, its body stretched to its full length just a foot or two above the sand. Again it landed on him and knocked the air out of his lungs.

In desperation, Carter grabbed at the enemy's wrists and hung on. The wrists were thin but wiry. A mass of soft hair blocked his vision, lashing at him like whips as its owner moved back and forth trying to free its wrists.

Signals reached Carter's brain from all over his body. He was still confused from hitting his head, but the signals were familiar and because of the familiarity, further confused his tired brain.

His chest told him that a pair of soft breasts were pressed against him. His thighs sent out the message that the thighs rubbing against his were familiar and exciting. His nose told him that the smell of the hair and the odors of the body were female.

"Wait!" he managed to croak out in the middle of the battle, just as a knee was reaching for his groin. *"Hold it!"* he rasped as he twisted to avoid the knee that caught him in his inner thigh, too close for comfort. "Just a damned minute!"

The woman on top of him stopped struggling. He brought her arms down to her sides but held on to the wrists. Then the tide of his emotions changed from battle to interest and something began to stir in his loins. Given time to examine her by the light of the stars, he found that she was beautiful. He released her wrists and she crawled away and stood in the pale glow of distant suns.

She was beautiful, indeed magnificent, a blonde about five feet eight, well proportioned, muscular, and a master of the martial arts. But what was she doing here? And why was she naked?

"Who are you?" he asked, rubbing the cut on the side of his head.

"Are you American?" she countered.

"As apple pie," he said. "Where did you learn to fight like that?"

"Can you get me out of here? They've killed my friends," she said, tears starting to roll down her cheeks, the shock of the encounter with him starting to take hold.

"You're Dr. Barbara Wall," he said slowly, wondering why he hadn't thought of it before. "I thought Zendal had you stashed away." He moved to the remains of his fire and sat, then motioned her to sit close by on a smooth rock that jutted from the sand.

"Who's Zendal?" she asked.

"I found the bodies of your friends. Zendal's people killed them. They captured me and I escaped."

"But who are you?"

"Nick Carter. The Canadian government asked our secretary of state for help in finding you. I'm it."

"You?" she said incredulously. "One man?"

He laughed. It started as a chuckle, not much more than a snort, and grew until it became a belly laugh that cleansed him of the threat he'd just escaped. It was good to laugh. It was equally as good to hear her join in as she watched him. The whole situation was so bizarre: he'd escaped alive from an undersea nightmare and was now on a deserted tropical island with a voluptuous nude blonde. Every red-blooded man's fantasy. . . . He wiped tears from his eyes, took a deep breath, and began his story.

He told the woman what had happened, leaving out not one detail or one assumption from the time he entered the first cavern until they met. She was a highly intelligent woman. She might be able to help. And most of all, if anyone had a right to know, it was she.

"It sounds like a bad dream. Is this the way you live all the time?"

"Between short vacations, in varying degrees, yes."

She thought about it for a moment and shook her head. "What I don't understand is, I believe every word. A mad scientist. They really do exist."

"You of all people should know it's possible," he said. "Here's one scenario. Take one of your colleagues, one of the most brilliant, frustrate him with constant funding problems and delays in approval for unusual experiments, take away his pride and sense of accomplishment, maybe even banish him because of his radical ideas. What is his recourse? A different university and the same problems all over again? A foreign government who will listen? I suspect this happens all too often," he went on, watching her face for a reaction.

"Where do you think he got the hundreds of malcontents I saw serving him?" he asked. "They all had to be dissatisfied. You can't tell me that you're not constantly short of funds and encouragement." He put another piece of driftwood on the fire and turned to her. "We treat our scientists like children and our politicians and military leaders like gods. In my opinion it should be the other way around."

"I think I'm going to like you, Nick Carter," she said, her smile something to behold. "But do you know what attracted me to you in the first place?"

"My sparkling personality?"

"Your excellent cooking. The smell of your food wafted across the whole island. I didn't trace the smell here until you'd cleaned up and sat back for a rest."

"Something tells me you're hungry," he said with a grin, rising to take the gear from his pack again. "Do you know how to catch fish here?" he asked.

"Never learned. You've got a pole and hooks?"

"No. You've got to use native techniques. Tell you what. You build up the fire and put some oil in the pot and I'll be back in a few minutes."

While he was gone it gave her time to think as she went through the menial tasks. She found dehydrated potatoes, peas, and corn in the pack, prepared them, and stirred them in a thin coating of oil. She could hardly believe they'd sent one man to rescue her whole expedition. But, she figured, that had to tell her something about him. True, he was big and strong and seemed competent. And—

she couldn't suppress a smile—he was a hell of a good-looking guy.

Carter returned with two fish still flapping on the end of a pointed stick. He took his sharp stiletto from his backpack and filleted the fish skillfully. He flipped the boneless pieces in the pan with the partially cooked vegetables and worked at her meal while she watched. In minutes, he covered her thighs with a half-dozen broad leaves, then scooped the whole pot of food onto a broad leaf and placed it on her lap.

"I'm going for a swim," he announced casually. "Fighting a female tiger in the sand makes a dip in a tidal pool sound like a distinct pleasure."

She sat and watched him as he swam to the coral reef that formed the tidal pool and joined him as soon as she was finished. They swam together for a few minutes, then walked side by side to a flat rock not far from shore and stretched out looking at the stars.

"There's something weird about all this," she said, the first one to speak.

"What's that?"

"We're both naked. We've never seen each other dressed."

"The natives in these islands didn't develop modesty until the missionaries came," he said.

"Did they make love often?" she asked.

"It was a natural function they indulged in every time the urge was upon them, and that was often. Civilization inhibits freedom of action, the act of doing what comes naturally."

"You're a very serious man," she said, turning on her side and raising herself on one elbow.

"And you are a beautiful woman. I can't imagine spoiling what you are by clothing you."

"Speaking of 'doing what comes naturally,' doesn't this night, this situation, make you feel like it's a good idea?"

"I have to admit, the thought has crossed my mind."

She laughed, a nice laugh, easy and real. "You have remarkable control, Nick Carter."

"A necessary ingredient in the art of love. A woman doesn't want to be thrown on the ground and ravished. She wants to be courted, admired, given self-esteem, and in the end, she wants to be loved tenderly—tenderly but thoroughly."

"Your knowledge of women seems pretty thorough . . ."

He reached for her. "I know a lot about life, Barbara, and women and love are a part of that . . ."

Their mouths came together and each reached for the other as if being close was the most important thing in the world. Her tongue teased his lips, begging for entry, and once inside, worked at his mouth like a warm serpent of love, bent on driving him wild. She built an urge in him so quickly that neither was interested in further foreplay. He rolled on top of her as she spread herself to receive him and found himself enveloped in a furnace that had been smoldering for hours.

She was as ready as he. The short battle and the magic of their island refuge acted as an aphrodisiac, forcing her to satisfy the heat of passion her body demanded—not in minutes from now, but right away. She clung to him, moved with him, and felt a climax coming that she knew instinctively they would both share.

It welled up within them both, urging them on, more like two combatants than lovers. They rolled on the sand and fought a battle for the prize that was so close, held so much promise, and was easily within their reach.

The wave of feeling, of excitement that was like an inner fire, consumed them as they lashed at each other, moving their loins in a cadence that was close to physical pain. The feeling persisted until they could not maintain the inhuman pace any longer. They started to savor the beginning of an afterglow that would last well beyond the pounding of hearts, the burning of lungs, the need to hold and smother each other with kisses of gratitude and wonder.

They lay still in the sand, still clasped as close together as was possible, until one hand moved to caress, a foot ran along a sandy thigh, a head moved to look into eyes that were half-closed with contentment.

"What was that?" Barbara sighed. "Where did it come from? That was extraordinary."

"It's this whole crazy situation," Carter reasoned. "You can't plan things like this."

"I've heard that violent death can drive those close to it to greater passion," she said, her voice deep and hoarse. "Oh, I don't know. I'm just overwhelmed. I've never experienced anything like it in my whole life."

He rolled to his side and looked down at her, at the golden halo of hair fanned out around her head, at the reflection of the stars in her hazel eyes, at the whiteness of her small, even teeth. She was a woman who would have brought out the best in him no matter the circumstance.

Her eyes met his, and her face broke into a smile. "I don't run into men like you every day. I'm usually surrounded by stuffy old men or overeager graduate students. I've never found academia to be a place for romantic fulfillment," she added, stretching in his arm, then rolling from him and running to the tidal pool.

He watched her run, her firm buttocks demanding his attention. He was about to jump up and follow her when the earth station came to life with the crackling of an indistinct voice.

He grabbed the push-to-talk handset and spoke as clearly as possible as he watched her break the water in a shallow dive. "N3. Say again. I didn't hear your opening message."

"Schmidt calling. Hold for him," a nasal-sounding voice came at him.

"Nick. Are you all right?"

Carter almost choked out a laugh but restrained himself. At that moment he was far better than all right. "I'll do. Where are you?"

"Passing your location on a regular sea-lane. I'm breaking away in a separate craft and should be there in two hours."

"Two hours. I hear you loud and clear. What kind of craft?"

"Pleasure boat. Don't worry about it. I've got it all worked out. I need a sheltered cove on the lee side of your island. South or north?"

"Try west. Fortunately, the lee side is the opposite side from Zendal's strange kingdom."

"Look for me in two hours. Over and out."

Carter put down the microphone and thought about his longtime friend. He didn't like to see AXE's records man, their resident genius with gadgetry, this close to danger. But he needed help and perhaps Schmidt had thought of something to stop Zendal.

His attention was caught by the splash of kicking feet as Barbara sprinted across the tidal pool. Instinctively he raced to the water and parted it in a racing dive. He swam underwater and grabbed her as she made a turn for another lap.

They came up out of the water gasping. Her mouth

sought his as he held her. The water came to his chest as his feet spread on the sandy bottom, providing a firm platform for the two of them.

She wrapped her legs around him and would not release his mouth. She moaned at the feel of him, knowing what was to come.

They had two hours of paradise before the reality of their goals caught up with them. They'd make the most of it.

EIGHT

At first all Carter could find in his pack for Barbara to wear was a tank-style undershirt. Standing in front of him, the fabric stretched taut by her thrusting breasts, she looked very sexy. They had seen Schmidt on the horizon and they had to get down to the cove to welcome him. To cover her lower half, the best he could manage was a pair of his "one size fits all" bikini briefs. They made her look even more sexy.

Hand in hand, they crossed over several ragged outcroppings of rock to a natural break in the sheer cliff face around the corner from the beach. It was wedge-shaped, a hundred feet deep and fifty feet across at its widest point. A shelf of rock, smooth as a billiard table, jutted from the cliffside ten feet from the water's edge.

Schmidt brought the fifty-foot Chriscraft in with the expertise that could only be gained from countless weekends spent sailing his own craft on the waters of the Potomac and Chesapeake Bay. The big man, grizzled by a fresh growth of beard, greeted Carter effusively then stared in amazed wonder at the scantily clad beauty at his side.

"This is Barbara Wall," Carter said, grinning like a kid showing off his new scooter. "*Doctor* Barbara Wall."

"I swear, Nicholas, you'd come up with a female companion if stranded in the Kalahari," he said, using Carter's full name as he did when he was either annoyed or too surprised to do otherwise. "But we obviously have to get her some clothes," he added.

"That can wait. Zendal's people had to see you coming in. We've got to do something to throw them off, camouflage this floating little palace."

"Say no more, old boy," Schmidt said, moving to the bridge. He pushed a button and an electric motor hummed. From the deck of the center cockpit, a hidden flap popped open and a strange-looking mast started to rise until it telescoped thirty feet over their heads. At the push of another button, the top of the mast started to open like a huge ungainly umbrella, thin steel ribs pushing cloth outward until the edges touched the rock on both sides and stuck as if glued.

"I told you about this character," Carter said proudly, grinning. "He's really something."

"An encore?" Schmidt asked.

"Yes, please," Barbara asked, smiling up at the cloth that was almost a mesh. It didn't keep out the sunlight but undoubtedly camouflaged the craft from anyone more than a hundred feet away.

While she ogled the huge cover with amazement, Schmidt flipped another switch and artificial palm trees sprang from several places on the huge canopy, their fronds moving naturally on the sea breeze.

"I have a meal fit for royalty ready in the galley, Nick, and your favorite Italian red. You want to eat or see some more Schmidt magic?"

"Let's see what you've brought," Barbara asked, clapping her hands like a kid waiting for Christmas morning.

"We'll get you some clothes first," Schmidt said, his eyes still on the bulges created by her breasts.

"To hell with clothes," Barbara replied. "Show us more of your inventions."

They followed him to the aft stateroom that had been stripped and converted to a launching area. It was dark. Schmidt didn't turn on any lights. They could see that pneumatic arms held the entire stern closed. While they watched, Schmidt lowered the steel sheeting of the stern to water level and the light revealed two undersea sleds unlike any Carter had ever seen. They were pointed at the bow, flat at the stern, and were driven by two cylinders each with an aft propeller. Above the flat surface of the craft, a half-dozen rocket mounts held projectiles of a type unknown to Carter.

"What are they?" he asked.

"You've heard of cluster bombs?" Schmidt said.

"Sure."

"I haven't," Barbara answered, fascinated.

"Cluster bombs can be dropped from the underbelly of almost any kind of aircraft. They can be set to explode any distance from the ground above a hundred feet. When they let go, they eject hundreds of small bombs that fan out and explode over the heads of the enemy," Schmidt explained.

"So what's the similarity here?" Carter asked.

"These can be set in the same way. They have three triggers each, twenty, fifty, and a hundred feet. You press a trigger and at the planned distance, they explode, sending hundreds of darts in an arc of ninety degrees."

Carter looked at his old friend with amazement. "I didn't know you dabbled in this kind of thing," he said.

"I don't normally. The odd small weapon that will help get an agent out of trouble, that sort of thing, but seldom anything like this."

"What made you do it?" Carter asked.

"A dream I had out on the Chesapeake one night.

Damned real, too. Saw you in hand-to-hand fighting underwater with a dozen men. Seemed unfair. I've been playing with this ever since."

"What made you bring it now? I thought you were just playing the big man with Hawk away."

"No such thing," Schmidt said indignantly. "I heard that your assignment was to find scientists who use underwater gear. I'd squirreled some AXE funds away for emergencies, and designed this boat and the sleds. The bombs were an afterthought. I almost didn't build them."

"What are these?" Barbara asked, pointing to equipment hanging from the walls.

"New kind of scuba gear. I talked to Cousteau about an improved version once. His idea. Don't know if he ever followed up."

"How do they work?" Barbara asked, taking one from the wall and putting her arms into the webbing like an expert.

"Double valve system. Each sled is atomic-driven. The power pack runs an oxygen plant similar to the ones used in space. You plug into the sled's supply when towed behind the sled. When you pull away, your own valve takes over and feeds from your own tank."

"What happens to the sled when you let go—if you have to leave it to attack or explore?" Carter asked.

"It goes to the bottom and sits, waiting," Schmidt answered proudly. "When you plug into its system again, the double valve inlet will recharge your tank."

"And if the water's very deep?"

"No problem. They sink very slowly."

"Fantastic!" Barbara said, hugging the big man.

"Now I *know* we have to get you some clothes," Schmidt kidded. "I've been locked away from specimens like you too long."

He took them on a tour of the boat. Even with the aft cabin used for diving, they still had a large master stateroom and two smaller sleeping rooms. "I'm in one of these," Schmidt said. "You two can do what you want with the other two. Every type of clothing is in the master stateroom. Why don't you explore while I dish out the food. Ten minutes, okay?"

When they came to the main salon in denim shorts and white shirts, the table was set for three. Glasses of ruby-colored Valpolicella were standing at each place, a pan of lasagna and one of cannelloni were in warming plates. Schmidt was in the process of dishing out a serving of each to them.

"My favorite food!" Barbara exclaimed, taking a forkful of the lasagna and washing it down with the earthy red wine. "My God," she went on, "this is wonderful, Howard. You're as amazing as Nick said and then some."

While they ate, they heard a patrol boat pass their position and keep going.

"One of Zendal's," Carter said.

"I'm surprised they couldn't smell the food," Barbara said, stopping only long enough to make the comment.

"The canopy filters out pollution and keeps odors in," Schmidt said casually. Then he brought the conversation to its core. "What's your plan?" he asked.

"I've got to get into Zendal's operation and act as one of them for a few hours," Carter said. "I'm not convinced all the people he's lured there are evil. Maybe the security people are, but not the scientists. I refuse to kill them all just to stop him."

"You're right. They could be under some hypnotic influence," Barbara offered, wiping her mouth with a napkin and pouring some more wine. "I can't believe so many responsible scientists would deliberately threaten our society."

"I'm convinced he's doping their food with something," Carter said. "I've got two jobs in his domain. One is to confirm that he's feeding them something, and the other is to sabotage his paging system to announce that they all have to get out. A bomb scare or something like that."

"But how will they get out?" Schmidt asked.

"Zendal always has at least two submarines loading or unloading. Empty of cargo and weapons, two subs can take them all out while he's busy with the destroyer."

"I can help with the sound system. I've got some remote-control electronics in my workshop aboard. The range can be increased to ten miles if need be."

"How would it work?" Barbara asked.

"Nick plants an announcement in their sound system. We can make one up in minutes. I've got a small remote-control recorder he can tap into their system. We trigger it anytime we want," Schmidt explained.

"Did you notify the admiral?" Carter asked.

"I did but he sounded skeptical."

"Can you get him for me now?"

"Why not? If he's there," Schmidt said, turning to a ship-to-shore set and spinning the dial. "Schmidt to U.S. naval base, Pearl Harbor. Urgent to Admiral Brenner. Code double yellow."

"What's double yellow?" Barbara whispered.

"Immediate. Your ears only."

"Jesus!" she said. "Little boys playing war."

Carter said nothing. It would be a futile argument. He waited for Brenner.

"COMPAC is ready," a detached voice came on. "Are you ready?"

"Put Brenner on," Carter said.

"Brenner," the line crackled. "That Schmidt again?"

"No. Nick Carter. Howard Schmidt was relaying my intelligence."

"That fits the pattern better. So I'm getting this from some superspook who works for an agency that no one has ever heard of. Great," he snapped into the radio, his voice filled with sarcasm.

"Listen carefully, Admiral. I've been in this madman's domain. He has weaponry you've never even dreamed of. He can take the *Lance* from you if you don't take immediate action."

"Stuff it, Carter. You're as crazy as the man you're trying to sell me. This whole story is utterly preposterous," he said as the line went dead.

Barbara and Schmidt had been listening on an external speaker. "Well!" she said disgustedly. "Is that what your military is like? My God! Are mine like that too?"

"Just a few who have egos too big for their heads," Schmidt suggested. "What are you going to do, Nick? We could get Hawk to go to the top on this one."

Carter had been working it out. It would take time to get to Hawk in transit, and the head man of AXE would have to get in touch with his contacts in Washington. Then they'd walk on eggs to avoid bruising egos at the offices of the Joint Chiefs of Staff. Brenner wouldn't get the message for days.

"No way we'll have time," Carter said. "I've got to infiltrate alone. But I'll need your help in planning. First things first—how am I going to get in?"

"There's no way you're going to go in alone. No damned way!" Barbara said hotly.

They both looked at her, surprised.

"I'm the expert on caverns here. If his place is as big as you say, he's got to have ventilators. I can find them more easily than you can."

"And I can give you metal detectors," Schmidt added. "Better both of you go than one."

"I run my own show, Howard. You know that. She stays."

"She goes," Barbara retorted. "Would you rather agree and have me accompany you, or would you rather I just followed?"

Carter had been up against stubborn women before and could seldom remember winning an argument. But, dammit, some of them had been killed in the process. Too many of them. He used that fact as an argument, but it didn't change her mind.

"I can probably handle the problem in the kitchen, the drug thing, while you handle the electronics. It'll take us half the time. In and out in a hurry. Better than you being exposed to twice—"

"All right!" he interrupted. "You win. But I'm not sure you should handle the drug angle. Someone will have to be persuaded to talk and that could take some muscle."

"And I don't have muscle?"

"I didn't mean it that way," he said, remembering the way they'd met all too well. "It might mean threatening death. Could you do that?"

She looked thoughtful for a moment or two. "I used to be a devout pacifist. But you can't let them push you around. They killed . . ." she said, her voice almost choking on the words.

"What about my drug pack?" Schmidt suggested. "You've used it often enough in the past."

"What's that?" she asked, her voice almost back to normal.

"Three drugs with small syringes in a neat package: one to use as a knockout tool, one as a truth drug, the last one lethal," Schmidt said.

"Christ, I'd hate to get them mixed up."

"So just take the truth drug."

Carter listened to them and resigned himself to the fact that she was going. Maybe she had a right. They'd killed her colleagues and tried to kill her. He'd seen the massive bruise on one side of her chest.

"I'll miniaturize a drug kit for you in a waterproof pack. Anything else?" Schmidt asked.

"Nothing I can think of right now. I don't like the idea of you being in the line of fire," he told his old friend.

"I won't be. I'm staying right here. Catch up on my fishing. Brought some gear along."

"No way. Stay inside this cover. That's a hard-and-fast rule. I'd feel better if you were out of it altogether."

"Hey. I'm not going outside this cover for a million bucks. Not yet, anyway. Just think of me sitting here by the rail, rod in hand, a cold beer at my side, and the radio on."

Carter laughed and got up to go to bed. "I think we'd all better get a few hours' sleep."

"I'm going to do the dishes and I'll be right along," Barbara said.

"No way, young lady. My ship, my dishes. You're no galley slave. Off to bed with you."

She followed Carter to the master stateroom and was about to close the door when the voice of AXE's resident genius boomed out behind her. "And try to get some sleep. At least an hour or two."

Inside the huge caverns that stretched through most of an underwater range heading away from the island base occupied by Schmidt and his sleek craft, Zendal sat in his throne room, his chief of security standing at attention in front of him. "You're telling me that our radar picked up a sizable blip breaking away from the freighter then disappearing from our screens? What about sensors? Did we pick up propellor noise?"

"Yes, Excellency," Schnieder answered. "Twin screws. A good-sized boat. We estimated her to be at least fifty feet, probably a pleasure boat."

"Estimated? Probably? What kind of answers are those? I want to know *exactly* what she was and where she went."

"But we've had every surface craft we own out looking for her, Excellency. She's just not there."

"Send them out again, fool!" he screamed at Schnieder. "What was her track when you heard her screws? When did you lose her? Scour that area again and again and if you don't find her, have the men crawl over every inch of rock within twenty miles of where you lost her."

"As you command, Excellency."

"You don't seem very enthusiastic," Zendal spat. "Let me catalogue your failures for you. First you permitted an enemy agent to infiltrate this installation. Next you permitted him to escape. You lost several tools in the process. You think I can produce new clones for you at a moment's notice?"

"No, Excellency."

"You told me that Carter did not survive your attack, but you never saw his body. I'd bet anything he's alive. I know his kind. He's out to destroy me. He'll be back and we must be alert for him. Now do you see why we can't just write off an unsuccessful search? *Find that boat for me or don't bother to come back!*"

When Schnieder had saluted and scurried from his presence, Zendal called in the man who controlled all his scientific personnel. "Report on our state of preparedness," he commanded.

"The U.S.S. *Lance* left Pearl Harbor at dawn this morning. She's headed our way. Taking her shakedown program into account, she should be here in about forty-eight hours."

"You know I don't like approximations," Zendal complained.

"Yes. I'm aware of your desire for precision," the chief of operations admitted. He was a man just past middle years, a German who spoke English precisely but with gutteral pronunciation. "But the *Lance*'s captain is allowed some latitude. We'll monitor her movements closely and we'll not be caught off guard."

"Good. Excellent. In forty-eight hours I want to see our magnetic field bring her closer to us. I want to see her go down," Zendal said, his eyes sparkling with anticipation.

"It will have to be a very accurate firing, Excellency," the scientist said. "We have to take her down while she's still on the Necker Shelf. If we miscalculate, she'll be in five thousand feet of water and we'd never get at her cargo before the navy'd be on to us."

Zendal scowled at the civilian. His ultimate goals would not permit approximations or brook failure. "If she goes down, if after all my planning you miscalculate, I'll use my escape hatch and flood this whole operation. You'll all die a horrible death, my friend—all of you."

The tall scientist, his hair almost white, walked from the room, his heart rate well above a hundred. *The bastard,* he thought. *The cold-blooded bastard.*

NINE

After they had rested, Carter and Barbara made their way to the main salon and found Schmidt in the process of taking platters of eggs, ham, and sausages from a warming oven. The smell of fresh coffee filled the luxurious living quarters and galley. The big man, freshly shaved and groomed, stood grinning at them, a special smile for Barbara. She and Carter had changed into thermal long johns that would be their only garments under the wet suits. The thin cloth showed off every line of her superb body.

"I know it's the middle of the night, but I've prepared breakfast," Schmidt said. "Sit and eat before you take off."

"Just coffee and a piece of toast for me," Carter said. "I don't like to go into action with a gut full of food."

"Well, I need the energy," Barbara said, sitting at one of the places and piling food on her plate.

"I've been doing a final check for you when you're ready," Schmidt said. "I've got more to show you about the sleds."

Carter was finished eating and sat with a cigarette and his second cup of coffee. He watched the woman fuel herself for the battle ahead. He sometimes wished he could

101

indulge himself in that way. But it had been ritual with him: a surfeit of food made him sluggish. Some people could burn off the excess energy easily, but he could not.

Schmidt sat, nursing his own coffee, never taking his eyes from the golden-haired woman between them. Carter was amused at the gadgets man he'd thought he could read like a book. He had never seen Schmidt completely dazzled by a woman, but then he usually saw the man in his own domain.

Barbara seemed to be unaware of either of them. Eating seemed to be as much a vocation as a necessity for her. Three eggs, two slices of ham, and a half-dozen sausages were pulverized by the perfect white teeth and disappeared into the seemingly bottomless pit that was her digestive machine.

Finally, Barbara dabbed at her mouth with a napkin and sat back, satisfied. "Let's see what you've done," she said to Schmidt, offering up one of her devastating smiles.

He led them back to the stern hold. They sat on bulkhead benches while he opened a sealed hatch on the portside cylinder. "The atomic motor takes up only a small part of the motor compartment. The forward section is lead-coated to compensate for the weight aft. It makes for an ideal storage compartment. Your gear can be stored in here—the drug case, Nick's personal weapons, dry-land clothing."

"What about communication?" Barbara asked.

"The hoods of your wet suits contain miniaturized transmitters," Schmidt explained. "They have two frequencies. On one you can communicate through the water. The range is low. On the other you can communicate with me. You'll have to surface to accomplish that. The range hasn't been fully tested, but it's at least ten miles."

"When we find the air vents, how do we get down them?" she asked.

"Most vents have internal ladders. If they don't, Nick will have a tool quite familiar to him—a thin wire around his waist with a grappling hook attached."

"And once down the vent, how do we get in?"

"We should be able to force their openings," Carter offered.

"And if you can't, I have these," Schmidt said, producing two strange objects. One looked like an oversize pen, the other more like a streamlined atomizer. "This one"—he indicated the penlike object—"is a torch. The other emits a fine spray of acid that will cut through alloys or aluminum but not steel." He gave each of them one of his small scuba tubes. "Use these for breathing while you cut through the metal."

"But we'll make noise in the process. We could be detected from inside," Barbara objected.

"The communications package built into your hoods has an attachment like a stethoscope," Schmidt answered, offering his best smile. "It would be a good idea to keep the hoods when you discard the scuba gear and wet suits."

Carter sat through the question and answer session quietly. Normally Schmidt would brief him and he would listen. It seemed natural for Barbara to be the one to ask questions. She wasn't a pro. Unlike Carter, she wasn't accustomed to improvising as the job progressed. "What's in the starboard motor casing?" he asked when Barbara appeared to have exhausted her questions.

"I'd prefer to save that until we have them on the run," Schmidt said, glancing at his watch. "It's past midnight. Now's the best time for your sortie. Any more questions?"

"I think we can take it from here," Carter said. "One thing. What are these jets on the motors?"

"Damn! I'm glad you reminded me," Schmidt said.

"The sleds normally cruise at up to twenty knots. But they have jet power. The accelerator is on your portside handle. Turn it clockwise and the jets burn in. They double your top cruising speed."

"Forty knots?" Barbara asked. "Is that safe?"

"Your suits are specially designed. Besides, it's safer than whatever's chasing you."

They put on their wet suits. Howard insisted on helping Barbara, showing her the earpieces for communication and the stethoscope looped around her neck.

Finally, Schmidt opened the stern bulkhead to a pitch-black night. "You have headlights but I don't recommend you use them. Zendal's island is on a bearing of zero-eight-zero degrees. You have a compass on your control panels. He's eleven miles from here by my calculations. At twenty knots you should reach there in a little more than thirty minutes. You have sonar on your control panel. Nick can figure it out."

The briefing had been thorough. All the equipment would be helpful and Schmidt's work had been superb. As they traveled side by side, getting the feel of the controls and testing the communications setup, Carter marveled at the sheer guts of the women he'd met. Barbara was special. Now that they were underway, he was happy she was with him. His job was highly specialized. Someone had to do it, but it was lonely. When you were out there alone, dependent on your wits and whatever weapons were at hand, it was like outer space, cold and uninviting.

He glanced at his sonar and saw that it was giving off signals that were twice as powerful as when they'd left. He glanced at his diver's watch and noted they'd been in the water for fifteen minutes. The two indicators checked out: they were halfway there.

At fifty fathoms the darkness was all-encompassing.

They were like pilots in a jet plane, totally dependent on their instruments. When the sonar read five degrees to maximum, Carter called to Barbara to cut speed to five knots and within minutes they saw the menacing base of the island.

They'd made it. From here on they would be working on dry land instead of in the black depths. Carter was about to start up the face of the rock when a half-dozen lights came at them out of the gloom.

"Maneuver behind me," Carter ordered. "I'm going to turn on my lights to see what we're up against."

They faced the enemy line astern when Carter turned on his powerful lights. Harpoons and spears bombarded Carter's sled as clouds of bubbles rose to the surface from gas firing mechanisms.

The enemy was firing first, asking questions later—if they had anyone left to ask. Carter was reluctant to use one of his cluster weapons but saw no alternative. He maneuvered until his sled faced the oncoming divers and pulled the trigger set for fifty feet.

He was not prepared for the result. In a split second, the bomb shot forward and released a cloud of darts just fifteen feet in front of the divers.

The darts were about six inches long. They looked like four saber-saw blades welded together, with six fins at the back to keep them on track. The field of fire at fifteen feet from release was about twenty feet in diameter. The darts hit five of the men that Carter could see. A cloud of blood filled the beam of his light and obscured his view.

Five of the six? He had to be sure.

"Stay where you are. Keep your lights off. We've got one on the loose."

"I'm not crazy about staying here alone," the reply came back. Barbara sounded scared for the first time.

"It has to be done. I'll make it as fast as I can."

He went to full power, his lights sweeping the water and rocks ahead. In seconds, he spotted the lone diver making for the cover of a jagged rock formation. Carter had to get him. They couldn't afford having Zendal know they were this close.

Twenty feet from the swimmer, Carter let go of the controls of the sled and swam. The Killmaster was smaller but more skilled. The size and shape of the diver looked like one of the clones. Zendal probably used them for all his most dangerous tasks.

Carter caught up with him and applied an iron-fisted hold to the man's temple. The clone tried to fight, but the hold rendered him unconscious in seconds. Carter ripped the hose from his mouth and left him floating free, starting to descend to the bottom.

The sled had also started to descend but had not traveled far. He turned it to catch up with Barbara only to find a school of hammerhead sharks vieing with smaller sand sharks for the bodies of the clones. The sea was a churning mass of blood and torn flesh in front of him. He shut off his lights, switched on his jets, and circled the feeding frenzy within seconds.

"Flash your lights just once," he ordered Barbara.

He saw the flash and turned toward the signal, keeping the sea around him dark. He didn't want to run into another patrol. They were undetected for the moment, but the patrol would be missed all too soon and these waters would be swarming with searching clones.

Carter didn't like the idea of their sleds floating to the bottom. He wanted them where he could retrieve them easily. He led Barbara closer to the rock and brought the sled to the surface.

The moon was out, a yellow ball amid a curtain of stars.

The island loomed above them. Carter led the way to a calmer area and found a shelf of rock just below the surface. He tied up his sled, picked out the tools he needed, and headed to the surface using his scuba gear.

Barbara followed. She scrambled up the rock face with more agility than he expected, despite being burdened by a metal detector and a pack that held the tools she would need.

As planned before they left, they fanned out, each with a metal detector, and started to sweep the rock face for a ventilator. Time dragged on for them. It was past two by the time Barbara signaled that she'd found a breather cap on a metal tube almost concealed by camouflaged Styrofoam that looked like the rock around it. The cap was welded to the tube. Zendal wasn't taking any chances.

They changed from scuba outfits to dry clothes and sneakers but kept the hoods and communication gear. The welding torch Carter carried peeled the top off the tube within minutes, leaving a ragged edge.

"Be careful. This edge is sharp," Carter told Barbara as he started down the wire rope he'd unwound from his waist. It was secured by a grappling hook that had looked like a Swiss army knife before he had opened all the prongs.

The descent seemed endless. He wondered if this would be their best avenue of escape. If they used any other exit, they wouldn't have their underwater gear and they might not find the sleds.

The vent seemed to go on forever. Carter could feel the swing as Barbara descended a few feet above him. All the while he descended, he could hear the ominous sound of a giant fan below. If their line parted, if they lost their grip, a multibladed meat grinder was waiting for them at the bottom.

Carter's flashlight picked out a door about ten feet above the blades of the fan. He signaled Barbara to stop while he investigated the opening. It was flanged at the edges, so he couldn't slip a probe in one side, but he soon discovered that the lock consisted of a single metal tongue holding the door. It was obviously connected to a locked handle on the other side.

First he pulled the stethoscope from around his neck and listened. He heard nothing but the roar of fans, the one serving his tube and several others not far away. He couldn't hear the ordinary sounds of human presence: a footfall, a cough, someone breathing nearby.

Carter pulled the torch from his pack and cut through the inch-wide tongue of metal that secured the door. He swung it open slowly, but saw nothing and heard nothing. He pulled himself through the two-foot-square opening and signaled for Barbara to follow.

The door was an entry used to clean the shaft or remove a foreign object. They were standing in a twenty-foot-square room surrounded by doors leading to other tubes. Carter pulled off his hood and hung it just inside the door. When Barbara had followed his lead, he shut the door and braced it. Then he moved to the door on the other side of the room and opened it a crack. No one was in the corridor outside.

"The action outside, the cluster weapon, it shocked you," he said, wanting to make sure Barbara could handle what was to come."

"I'm not exactly used to. . . . When my friends were killed I panicked. . . . I'll be all right."

"Good girl. The guards are all mindless, almost like robots. We have to think of them as robots," he explained. "They're expendable. If we're to save the others, we can't be squeamish about killing the guards.

"Are you all right?" he asked before he opened the door.

"I'll do. I see the logic, but I'm not a killer," she said, palming the silenced Beretta Schmidt had given her. "I told you before, I was a confirmed pacifist until Zendal killed my colleagues. Strange. I never thought I'd ever change."

Carter could empathize with the woman. She'd been through hell. But the job wouldn't wait. He took off his small backpack and flipped it open. He put on a white lab coat over his shirt. His Luger was in place under his left armpit and his stiletto was in its sheath on his right forearm. Barbara followed suit and slipped the Beretta into her waistband.

"Okay. We try to contact the scientists first. We need intelligence and identification," Carter said.

They moved down a corridor toward a door showing light through a crack at the bottom. Carter waved her behind him, turned the handle, and moved into the room with blinding speed.

They were in a dimly lit laboratory. Partly completed clones lay on stone tables, bionic arms and legs next to them ready for installation. Chests moved in unison as human hearts beat out a steady rhythm. Eyes followed them around the room but nothing was said, no alarm given.

"It's horrible," she said, her hand to her mouth.

"Maybe it's just as well you saw this," he said, keeping his voice as low as possible. "Remember this assembly line when the time comes to defend yourself from them."

They moved as silently as possible to the next door. Carter swung it open and they were both inside in a fraction of a second.

Two clones sat at a bank of video screens. Unlike normal humans, they didn't hesitate or show surprise. They were out of their chairs and heading toward Carter almost as fast as he had entered.

Carter sidestepped the first clone, and Hugo's needle-sharp blade slid between the ribs of the second one. Before Carter could turn back to the twin of the dying clone, the giant with a steel grip had the AXE agent by the throat in a death hold.

As red spots flashed in front of his eyes and the stiletto clattered to the floor, Carter heard a coughing noise and the hands left his throat. He slipped to his knees, still dizzy, and saw Barbara, her gun in hand, pointing the smoking muzzle at the clone. Mortally wounded, the creature fell against Carter, knocking him over.

"Are you all right?" Barbara asked, pulling the dead guard from him.

"I'm okay," he said, reaching for Hugo. She looked better than she had a few minutes earlier. The action had been a steadying influence instead of a shock. Good. She was going to be all right.

Carter put her out of his mind for the moment and scanned the wall in front of him. A schematic of the whole underwater installation was spread out and labeled. "Look at this," he said, motioning her forward. "A lot of the space is partitioned off. The scientists' quarters are here." He pointed to a section of the board. "It looks like we're here."

"Not very close," she sighed.

"We didn't think this was going to be easy. Let's get going."

They moved from hallway to hallway, trying to look happy and confident, as if they had every right to be there. They were almost to the civilian quarters when they were stopped.

This time neither of them hesitated. As soon as the two suspicious guards asked their identities and started to unsling their rifles, one took a slug in the chest from the Beretta and the other a stiletto in the heart.

"There's a storage room here," Barbara whispered to him, holding the door while he dragged the muscular clones inside.

"We've got to keep going," he urged. Before they moved on, he mopped blood from the floor with one of the light blue tunics worn by all the clones.

The civilian quarters looked the same as all the other rooms leading off all the corridors. They were simply numbered.

"What we need is one couple. We try to get through to them, to have them act as a conduit to the others. And we need identity badges," he said, his hand on the doorknob of the first door on the right.

A man slept alone in a bed in the far corner.

"This could be the single quarters," he whispered as he closed the door.

Barbara tried a door on the other side. A couple was sleeping in a double bed in the room. The quarters were Spartan. In addition to the bed, two chairs, a dresser, one mirror, and one picture was all the room contained.

"Put your hand over the woman's mouth and the gun to her head," Carter ordered as he flipped Hugo into his right hand and pressed the tip to the man's neck. "Wake up," he hissed in the man's ear. "And don't move or you're dead."

The man came out of a deep sleep with a start that pushed the stiletto into his skin. The wife's eyes were wild above Barbara's slim hand.

"Be still and we won't hurt you," Carter said as calmly as he could. He nodded to Barbara. "It's all right. Take your hand away."

"Who are you?" the woman spoke first, terrified.

"Agents of the United States government sent to rescue you," Carter said.

"From what?" the man asked, sincerely confused.

"Surely you know. Zendal is a threat to the whole world. He plans to steal atomic weapons and blackmail the United States and other powers," Barbara added.

"That's nonsense," the man scoffed. "Dr. Zendal is a genius. The fools who run governments don't appreciate his contributions to science."

"You'll go on working for a man who intends to sink an American naval vessel to steal nuclear weapons?" Barbara asked. "What kind of people are you?"

Carter waved he off. "Give me the leather case and keep your gun on them," he ordered.

He administered a dose of the knockout drug that would keep them out for a few hours. "It's no use," he told her as he worked. "They can't see our logic, not until the mind-controlling drug he's got them on wears off. We take their badges and do what we came here for," Carter said, packing the syringes back in the case and putting it in the pocket of her lab coat. "Do you remember which is the truth drug?" he asked.

"No problem," she said. "According to the layout we saw, the kitchens are on the next level not far from here."

"I've got a little further to go. I'll meet you back at the air vent in an hour. We can't afford to take any longer," he told her.

"See you there," she said, heading for the door.

"Barbara," he called her back. "Pick a chef who sleeps alone, preferably older than the others. And he can't be left around to warn Zendal you've neutralized his drug."

"What the hell does that mean?"

"Howard's truth drug is very rough on the heart. An overdose will bring on a fatal heart attack."

"I'm not sure I can do that," Barbara said, a tear coursing down her left cheek.

Carter took two steps to her and held her to him. "I never kill unless it's absolutely necessary," he whispered in her ear. He stroked her back while she settled down. "If the chef notifies Zendal's people, everyone here will die with him eventually. We've got to free hundreds."

"But can't I use the knockout drug . . . ?"

"He might have to be out for forty-eight hours or more," Carter reminded her. "It's not enough."

"I was able to shoot when . . . you know . . . when you were in danger . . . the clones. But this is so—so cold-blooded."

"I know," Carter said softly. "But the chef probably knows what he's doing to these people. He's probably doing it for money . . . the same kind of thinking that would condone the deaths of your friends just because they got in the way."

She was silent for a full minute, breathing heavily in his arms.

"Look, Barbara, I didn't want you to be subjected to this in the first place. Wait for me at the air duct and keep our avenue of escape clear."

"No," she said emphatically. "I said I'd do it and I will."

He raised her face to his so he could look her in the eye. The hazel eyes were rimmed with red from the emotions she'd gone through, but the set of her jaw was firm.

"Let's do it," she said.

TEN

The corridors looked like many Barbara had used before, prefabricated sections that joined easily but looked sterile. Not far from the room she'd just left, a red exit sign drew her attention. She opened the door to a stairwell.

In the reduced light, she glanced at the identification badge she wore. She was Dr. Ruth Marshall. The picture wasn't even close.

What the hell was she doing here? she asked herself as she climbed the stairs. Everything seemed so unreal. It was almost impossible to conceive that she was a thousand feet below sea level searching for a chef with the prospect of killing him.

Luckily she met no one as she opened a door to the floor at the next level and looked around. It was the middle of the night. Guards would be on duty but it would be a skeleton staff. If she was lucky she might finish her piece of business without running into anyone.

Barbara had no doubt that she was near her objective. She could smell the kitchens, the unmistakable odor of recently cleaned sinks, scrubbed pots, scraps of food in inaccessible places. What she didn't know was whether the chefs slept nearby. It had only been an assumption. She should have asked Ruth Marshall if she knew.

She tried a door. The hinges protested and a man turned over in his sleep. The room smelled of stale food, the badge of the kitchen worker. The room was small and untidy, not what you'd expect from the head chef.

Three more rooms looked the same. She'd tried them all but did not find the man she wanted. But the kitchens were next to the door she'd tried last. She wandered through the dimly lit space, past the stainless steel sinks, the cutting blocks, the rows of hanging pots that cast eerie shadows against the tiled walls.

On the far side she found an office, glanced at the paper, and found that they were invoices for food and utensils. The office of the man she sought.

A door led off the office and she tried it. A man slept in a much bigger bedroom. A night light plugged into the wall near another door showed the interior of a bathroom.

The man turned on his back and started to snore. The intake and outflow of air produced a worse noise than a pig at a trough. The huge mound of the man shook with each breath and the glass at his bedside, half-filled with a green liquid that contained his teeth, jiggled, the liquid constantly on the move.

This was her man. She closed the door and locked it. The leather case containing the syringes, though small, was heavy in her hand. She opened it and filled a syringe with Schmidt's own brand of truth serum.

The obese man on the bed appeared to be a perfect candidate for a heart attack even without her help, Barbara thought as she put the vial of fluid back in its compartment.

Barbara Wall put the syringe on a side table. She pulled the Beretta from her belt, placed the barrel against the sleeping man's forehead, and applied pressure.

One eye opened and then the other. The round, bloated face started to wrinkle as he screwed up his features in fear. The smell of urine filled the room. The man had a weak bladder which explained the night light and the open bathroom door. It didn't help. Barbara guessed she was probably far more afraid than he.

"I'm not going to hurt you if you cooperate," she said, taking one of his hands in hers and bending the wrist back. "Not any more than necessary," she added, knowing it was a lie.

The chef let out a moan as his wrist screamed at him for relief. It was a favorite police hold for moving unwilling prisoners. When they were standing, it usually brought them up on their toes. In the bed, the man could do nothing but endure.

"Turn over on your stomach," Barbara ordered, still holding the wrist bent backward.

He moved gingerly, favoring his wrist, trying to ease off the pressure.

When he was on his stomach, his face partially in his pillow, the moaning stopped and he started to cry. "Don't hurt me . . . don't kill me . . ." he pleaded.

"Where do you hide the drug you are feeding the people here?" she asked, hoping there was some way she could avoid killing him. She crammed the gun back in her belt and reached for the syringe.

"I don't . . . I don't feed them. . . . Don't hurt me, please," he whined, dragging out the last word in a plea for mercy.

She held the syringe vertical to purge it of air, although it didn't really matter if she gave him an embolism, then plunged it home in the fatty part of his upper arm.

He jerked and cried out, "You've killed me! What have you . . . ?" The question dragged out as his body sagged.

She released his wrist and with great difficulty managed to turn him over.

Barbara had no experience with interrogation, but she'd once seen a truth drug used by a psychiatrist. The first question he'd asked was the patient's name. Perhaps it was some kind of test.

"What is your name?" she asked.

"Benjamin . . . Benjamin . . ."

"Your full name?" she asked.

"Salter. Benjamin Salter."

She relaxed for the first time in hours. The door was closed. The others were asleep, it was the early hours of the morning, and she'd done the hardest part.

"All right, Benjamin. Listen to my voice and tell me why you are here. Why are you a chef here?"

"Why?" he seemed to ask himself. "They pay me."

"They pay more than others?"

"More. Danger pay."

"But you have to do something for the money. What else do you have to do?"

"Just feed them all. Feed the workers. Feed the guards. Feed the other chefs, all the domestics, and feed the master and his people."

She hesitated before asking the next question. His face had started to take on a rosy hue. His breathing was ragged. "You feed the workers something special, don't you. Very clever. It keeps them in line so they'll do what the master wants."

"What the master wants," he repeated, his breathing labored, his forehead wet with sweat, his hands clawing at his chest.

"Where do you keep it?" she asked anxiously. She didn't like the look of him. "What do you put in their food?"

"Flour. Extra flour. Can on top shelf. Spiked with something Zendal gave me."

"What color is it? What does it look like?" she asked desperately as his face started to register severe pain.

"Red can. Red metal can."

"Do the others know, the men who work with you?"

"Fools," the man said, settling down in the bed, his hands at his sides, the bedclothes soaked in his sweat. "They are drones. What would they know?"

She brought a washcloth she'd soaked in cold water to his bedside and started to wipe his forehead. He was still. Too still. She put her hand to the carotid artery at his neck and found no pulse.

"Oh, God!" she moaned, sinking to her knees. "I've killed him!"

Carter walked through the corridor quickly, giving the impression of a man with a mission. His identity badge was no better than Barbara's. Dr. Frank Marshall was bald. Carter had taken a moment to doctor the photo but it hadn't helped much.

The communications center was almost at the heart of the huge installation, much further than Barbara had traveled to her assignment. Carter memorized every turn in the labyrinth of corridors he traversed to get to his goal. He met only one guard and the big man, the clone, ignored him. The next question was who would be in the room at this time of night and whether he could pull off his magnificent bluff.

The endless corridors of prefab sections finally ended with one huge room in the cavern that Carter had seen before. The communications room was a huge glassed-in enclosure on a kind of mezzanine floor. It could be reached from a circular steel stairway leading from the cavern floor. Carter would be visible from the moment he stepped into the main cavern until he was in the glass enclosure.

The hairs rose on the back of his neck. They had always been a sure warning to him that he was being observed. They were one reason he wasn't a lover of technology related to his unique talents. This uncanny sixth sense had saved his life more than once, but it didn't work with video cameras or electronic listening gear.

He reached the bottom of the circular stairs and began to climb. No one stopped him. He wasn't challenged until he entered the communications center and faced two scientists on duty.

"Who are you?" one of them asked, looking up from a technical manual. He had a video monitor stripped down on a workbench.

"Frank Marshall," he answered without hesitation. "Where's the public address system?"

"Where'd you come from?" the man persisted. The other technician looked up from his work on an electronic circuit board and said nothing.

"Came in today. Supposed to add a few automatic announcements to the system," Carter said, flashing the small tape machine in front of the first technician. "An order from His Excellency."

"The far wall, second shelf," the man said.

Carter didn't speak again but went about his business. When he was finished wiring in the tape machine, he sensed the first technician at his shoulder.

"What are you doing?" the man asked.

"An announcement His Excellency can activate by remote control when he's ready. Some kind of evacuation procedure," Carter said, knowing the closer his story was to the truth the better chance it had of flying.

"Evacuation?" the other man said. "I guess that makes sense. We'll have to get the hell out of here when it's all over," he said, moving back to his bench.

"When what's all over?" Carter asked.

"You weren't told?"

"No."

"Then you weren't intended to know. That's the way it works around here, buddy, and you'd better get used to it."

"Worse than the fuckin' army," Carter said, trying to stay in character.

"Just don't let them hear you talking like that. Hey— where are you going?" the technician asked. He was the only one of the two to speak, obviously the senior man.

"I'm not really on duty," Carter said. "It just bothered me that that small job wasn't done."

"Just don't get too damned efficient," the man said. "It'll make us all look bad. You get the message?"

"Sure. Sorry. I got the drill. You get what you pay for, right? No more, no less."

"You've got it. See you at chow later."

The mention of food turned Carter's thoughts to Barbara. "What time's breakfast?" he asked as he opened the door to the stairway.

The man looked at his watch and Carter glanced at him. "Six o'clock. An hour and a half."

An hour and a half. . . . Barbara could be finishing up just as the kitchen help came on duty, he thought. He headed down the stairs and crossed the huge amphitheater of the cavern with a frown on his face.

"The Killmaster, I presume," a voice behind him said, the sarcasm evident in the tone.

Carter whipped around, his Luger in his hand, to find Zendal surrounded by a half-dozen clones, each with a rifle pointed at him. He already knew that their reaction time was almost a match for his own. By the time he got off one shot, they could fill him with steel from six rifles firing more than seven hundred rounds a minute. He might kill Zendal, but he would be dead and Barbara would be stranded. It was too high a price to pay. He decided to live and fight another day.

On her knees, the huge dead man before her, Barbara Wall was conscious of sounds behind her. The sous chefs, the dead man's assistants, were up already and starting to prepare the morning meal. She cursed under her breath. What the hell was she supposed to do now?

She looked in the bathroom mirror. An idea occurred to her. She undid her long blond hair from the bun she'd worn while in action and it fell to her shoulders in disarray. She ran her fingers through it, rebuttoned her lab coat so that it was buttoned wrong, and started for the door.

She had another idea halfway across the room and returned to the bed. With distaste she pulled the pajama bottoms from the huge rump, leaving him naked from the waist down. She unbuttoned his top and moved to the bathroom for a couple of towels. She arranged them in two crumpled heaps on the floor beside the bed, then stepped back to survey her work. A sated man if she'd ever seen one, a man too played out from an all-night orgy to get to work on time.

The lock made a loud click as it turned in her hand. Every man on the staff, four of them, stood looking at the door as she crept out and closed it slowly behind her, giving them a glimpse of the man on the bed.

The men stood, mixing spoons in hand, white hats towering to the ceiling, grinning at her.

"I'm supposed to inspect the condiments," she said, moving to the shelf the dead man had indicated.

"What department are you from?" one of the men

asked, a lascivious grin on his face. "You work strange hours."

"Medical department," she snapped back at him, making an effort to button her coat properly and running a hand through her hair self-consciously. "Got to inspect the kitchens once a month."

"Ain't never heard of no inspection," another of the cooks offered. He wasn't the brightest of them and hadn't caught on to the gag.

"Spot checks," she shot back at him.

"And what were you inspecting in the chef's bedroom?" the first man asked, almost at the point of laughter.

"This and that," she said, looking him in the eye, maintaining eye contact until he turned away.

She found the red canister she sought and tasted it with one finger. She was positive she'd found the right one. "This flour's got maggots in it," she said, dumping the contents into a slop pail where it sank to the bottom through a mass of coffee grounds, rendered fat, and eggshells.

"Your boss asked me to tell you he's sleeping late," she added as she headed for the corridor. "I'm sure you can manage without him," she said, smiling for the first time, and, in the process, giving the acting performance of her life.

Sweat poured down her back, dampening the lab coat as the door closed behind her. She could hear a hoot of laughter from the kitchen and had to grin to herself as all the men joined in.

The route back to the air vent was burned in her memory. If Carter was waiting, they'd be able to get out of there right away. *Please, God, make him be waiting,* she said to herself. If she was first, she didn't know if her nerves could stand the pressure. As she rounded a corridor, intent on her thoughts, a group of clones were leading

Carter in their midst. A man she assumed to be Zendal was bringing up the rear.

Barbara went for the Beretta, but one of the clones brought the butt end of his rifle up and clipped her on the chin. She went down hard, hitting her head on the floor.

Carter regained consciousness and felt the pounding inside his head. The scene came back all too clearly. When Barbara had gone down, he'd moved to help her and that was the last thing he remembered.

He tried to focus on his situation. His wrists were tied together and he was naked, strung up so that the soles of his feet could barely touch the floor. He was tied at the lower back and below his buttocks to a moving object, like him, swinging from a rope.

It was Barbara. They were lashed together, naked. Her head was to one side, lolling from a rubbery neck, her eyes closed.

"Barbara," he called. *"Barbara."* He tried to move against her, to bring her out of it, but he'd have to wait until she was ready.

Slowly she opened her eyes. "Oh-h-h-h, my head," she moaned. Then she realized she was tied, naked, to another human. "My God!" she gasped. "What the hell . . . ?"

"Don't be bashful. We've got to get out of this and it's going to take all our wits."

"All my wits hurt," she mumbled.

Suddenly the door swung open and Zendal strode in, followed by someone who wasn't a clone. He appeared to be in charge of the clones. Perhaps the chief of security, Carter thought.

Barbara fell against him, limp, her eyes closed.

"Cut them down," Zendal ordered. "Put the woman on the table. Hold the man so he can watch."

They cut the two of them down and the restored circulation pained his extremities. But it was better than being hung like a side of beef. He stood between two clones. Their grip of steel held him while Zendal went to work on Barbara.

Zendal poured a glass of water and held it to her lips. She blinked her eyes and looked at him. When full realization hit her, she opened her mouth in a silent scream and tried to cover her nakedness with her arms and hands.

"What have you done with my clothes?" she demanded.

Carter stood and admired her. She was creating exactly the atmosphere he wanted. If the clones were normal they'd be intent on her, but they stared straight ahead. The effect on the chief of security was different, however. The lush body, the breasts swinging free, had him in the grip of his own private fantasies.

"Schneider, bring the tray," Zendal said.

Schneider didn't move. His eyes were riveted on the hand covering her crotch.

"Get the damned tray, I told you!" Zendal screamed at him.

The man dragged his eyes from the woman reluctantly and brought a tray of syringes to a small table beside Zendal, then his eyes went back to their area of interest.

Zendal prepared a syringe and held it up for Carter to see. "You know what this can do, don't you. She'll tell us all she knows and she'll end up a vegetable. Why don't you save me the trouble, Carter?"

"She doesn't know anything. It's a waste of time."

Barbara timed it perfectly. She brought her hand from her crotch and grasped Zendal by the elbow. With the other hand she plunged the drug into the man's arm and slipped from the table.

Carter had a feeling something of the kind was coming

and broke loose from the clones as their grip loosened. He cartwheeled and caught each man in a karate heel chop while Barbara was using her best moves on the one called Schneider.

Carter went for his Luger in a pile of clothing near the door. Barbara had her Beretta in her hand almost as quickly. One of the clones, almost recovered, went for Carter and two 9mm slugs from Wilhelmina blew off the top of his head. While Carter was zeroing in on the second clone, he heard two coughs from the Beretta and the sound of bullets plowing into yielding flesh.

As the second clone slid down the far wall, a 9mm hole in his heart, Carter turned to see Barbara, blond hair askew, hazel eyes flashing, and smoke again seeping from the lowered automatic.

"Let's get out of here," he grunted, starting to dress.

"It's crazy. I don't feel the least bit guilty," she said.

"Get dressed and let's get out!" he urged her. "We don't have time right now for editorials."

ELEVEN

Barbara headed for the door and into an empty room down the corridor, her clothes bundled in her arms. Carter followed her. They dressed in the dark while noises in the corridor told them their handiwork had been discovered.

Carter felt one hell of a lot better with his weapons in place and his enemy temporarily out of the picture. If he could have killed Zendal before Barbara took off it might have saved them a lot of trouble, but he had to think of the hundreds of innocent people still trapped in the undersea prison.

They had to hurry. The place was swarming with Zendal's clones and more would arrive as the word went out. They stepped out into the corridor, asked a sleepy couple what was happening, and joined the crush of curious for a few seconds until they had blended into the scene. Then they slipped away in the direction of the ventilation shaft.

"Zendal's security people will have the rock surrounded with divers," Carter warned. "We've got to get to the sleds as quickly as possible."

"I'm right behind you," Barbara said, her voice showing her fear. Carter could understand the emotion. It would be unnatural if she weren't afraid. The question was whether she could hold up under the strain.

"Where are you going?" a metallic voice behind them asked.

Carter turned to see a clone bringing his rifle into play. The report of Barbara's Beretta sounded like a cannon in the narrow confines of the hall. It would be heard for hundreds of yards. While the clone dropped his weapon and crumpled to the floor, Carter grabbed her arm and hustled her along, thinking about the question he'd just posed to himself. She'd given him the answer in spades, had reacted as he would himself in the emergency. She was all right, better than all right. It was strange how some people could rise to tackle any situation in an emergency while others fell on their faces.

His musings didn't keep them from making good time. As they rounded the last corner near their escape shaft, he had to let go of her hand and bring Wilhelmina into play in one fluid motion. He took out one clone with a shot to the head and a security man with a clean shot to the heart. As they passed, the clone was sliding down a partition wall, his fluids spilling on the tiled floor, multicolored hydraulic fluids mixed with blood. In the microsecond of time that the sight registered on the Killmaster's brain, they were past and in the room containing the root structure of the vents.

Barbara paused, confused by the number of shafts that faced them. Carter moved with purpose and opened the door he'd marked with a star scratched in the paint.

"Put on your wet suit hood so we can communicate," he called to her from inside the shaft. "And be careful of the damned fan. It's still at full revs."

He was using Howard Schmidt's communications system now. "You read me all right?" he asked.

"Perfect," she said as she climbed in beside him.

They had to press their ankles against a small ridge just above the fan. Without their hoods they wouldn't have been able to exchange a word.

"You go first." He passed her a pair of gloves not unlike those worn by golfers. "Take every handhold carefully and try not to slip. The wire can be tricky—rip the skin right off you."

She started up the shaft slowly, gaining speed as she neared the halfway mark. Carter waited until she gained confidence before adding his motion to the wire. He sounded the panel with his stethoscope before starting up. Someone was in the room outside. He took a firm hold of the wire and started up.

Barbara Wall had never been so afraid in her whole life. What the hell kind of life did Nicky lead? She'd known he was an intelligence agent when they'd been alone on the island—she let her mind dwell on the excitement and adventure of it for a second or two—but she'd never imagined anything like this. The first real shock had been the devastation of the cluster bomb when it tore the five clones apart. Since then, one violent act had followed another. How could anyone live like this?

Her mind not on the job at hand, she slipped a foot down the thin wire, pressing her knees and toes against the tube and watching as blood trickled from the gloves he'd given her.

"Watch it, Wall," she muttered, then realized anything she said would be transmitted to Carter.

"How are you doing?" he asked.

She knew he'd like her to move a lot faster but didn't want to spook her. She appreciated it. "I'm all right," she responded, then heard him curse.

"Get the hell up as fast as you can!" he said, his words followed by the bark of his Luger.

"What's going on?" she called to him, trying not to panic and taking the wire hand-over-hand almost at the top.

At first he didn't answer. She heard two more shots and the rip of an automatic rifle. It sounded far away. No bullets came at her from below. But Carter was between her and the enemy.

"Are you all right?" she called, her breath ragged from the last effort to reach the top.

"I'm fine. But we've got to get into our wet suits and move the sleds out of here *fast*," he said as he climbed out of the top of the tube after her. "Your hands are bleeding," he added, noting the blood dripping from her torn gloves. "Here. Put my gloves on over yours. We can't have blood trailing after us in the water. Sharks can detect and follow the slightest amount."

Carter pulled on his wet suit and watched to be sure Barbara was right behind him. She had her suit on and was pulling on her air tank webbing. When he was ready for the water, he checked her over and found her long training was coming into play. She was as ready for the water as he. He didn't like to enter unfamiliar water near shore headfirst or even rolling in backward as he might from a diving platform. He cannonballed from a shelf of rock, his legs tucked beneath him, making the entry as shallow as possible. His judgment was sound. His feet hit another shelf a few feet below the surface but not hard enough to do damage. He saw her follow him a few feet away, and when the bubbles had cleared, he knew that she too was all right.

The sleds had to be close by, a few feet under the

surface. He used his flippers for motion while he held his flashlight in front. He could see light following along behind.

At the sleds, he came across two clones examining them, starting to take hold of the grab rail and reaching for the controls.

"Cut your light," he said to Barbara, "and stay put."

By the time he had arrived with his stiletto in his hand, the sleds were untied and floating free. The clones were trying to figure out how to start them.

Carter came in from below, keeping in mind the almost superhuman strength of these creatures. The long thin knife flashed once and the sea was filled with blood from a severed artery. It looked like a black cloud in the dim light and almost obscured the other figure. He had turned from the sled and had his gas weapon trained on the Killmaster.

Carter whirled in the water, diving below the cloud of blood as a harpoon flashed past his head. He came up on the clone's side, hidden by the black cloud, and brought the knife up in a flashing arc to skewer the big man between the third and fourth rib on the left side of his chest.

The two masks were less than a foot apart. Carter saw the look of surprise in the inhuman eyes and the beginning of death. He didn't waste any time in the shark-infested waters. "It's all clear! Get your sled and let's get the hell out of here!" he shouted.

Barbara was with him in seconds, her sled started and turned toward the island, where Schmidt and his yacht waited for them.

"Follow me," Carter said. "I'm taking a bearing of one-ninety degrees. We'll make a wide sweep and come in on Howard when we're sure we haven't got a tail."

"I can see you. I'm—"

There was sudden silence. Carter turned to see her behind him and slightly to the right. A small shark had her by the leg and was tugging at the limb, trying to tear off a hunk of flesh.

"I see you, Barbara! Can you talk?" He could see other sharks closing in while he talked.

"He's got my flipper but I can't do anything about it! He's . . . he's got too much strength!"

"Go to your boosters. Make sure your mouthpiece is in firmly and go to full power."

He waited, watching the battle unfold. The shark, no more than three feet long, was trying for a bigger mouthful. As it opened its jaws to lunge ahead, the sled took off and his razor-sharp teeth closed on the end of her flipper. As she gained speed, almost out of sight, the rubber came away in the shark's mouth.

Carter boosted his sled and hung on as it went to what felt like Mach 1. "You okay?" he asked.

"Is that physically or mentally?" she came back at him.

"You'll be all right," he said. "Let's try for one-ninety degrees for a few minutes and come back to our island at normal speed."

At well over forty knots, they passed a half-dozen swimmers, clones, who turned but didn't attempt to give chase. Good. The enemy would have a bearing on them that was entirely false. When they were well out of sight, he ordered a turn to the west and finally led her in toward their island and the stern of Schmidt's boat.

With Barbara shoveling roast beef, potatoes, and salad into her mouth in a steady stream, Carter brought Schmidt up to date on their sortie.

"Too bad you couldn't have killed the bastard while you had him," Schmidt said.

"Too many unknown factors. We know he's got several hundred valuable citizens under his control. And I couldn't have been sure he didn't have a second in command who would kill them all if I got Zendal."

"How do you balance them off against a new navy ship and its crew?"

"Dammit, Howard. I'm not God. The ship is expendable. The crew might be saved, or most of them. They're professionals. The scientists are the victims."

"He's right," Barbara offered between mouthfuls. "What about Brenner? He'll be tracking the new ship. He could be on the scene in hours."

"I'm counting on it," Carter said. "If Zendal follows his plan, he'll cut the ship at the waterline. I can't see high casualties. Brenner's support ships should be here in time to rescue the crew."

"The timing will have to be perfect," Schmidt said. "Let me tell you the way I see it and if we agree. You two will have to be ready with your sleds not far from the ship when she's hit. You signal me and I'll trigger the announcement for the scientists to get out."

"That's it in its simplest form," Carter said. "But I'm concerned about you. I don't like leaving you here. You'll be vulnerable as hell if some of Zendal's scouting parties finally see through your camouflage."

"But I won't be here, Carter," Schmidt said, and grinned. Then he held up a hand for silence. "I've got sensors out on the island. They're signaling. We've got a large party of intruders poking around."

"Can you tell how many?" Barbara asked.

"Not precisely. Between five and ten. Closer to ten," Schmidt announced.

"Do you have any kind of an arsenal on board?" Carter asked.

"Not much. A silenced M-14 sniper's rifle. Used by SWAT people a lot. It's sometimes used as an assassin's tool. Put a full clip of thirty rounds inside a five-inch circle at two hundred rounds. Before I got to fiddling with it, they called it the XM-21."

"What else?" Carter asked, impressed with the M-14. "I might be able to take care of them with the rifle, but what if they're out in real force and bunched up?"

"I adapted the M-16 grenade launcher to the M-14. I can attach it if you want. It's not exactly a silent weapon."

"Good enough," Carter said, pulling off his wet suit and replacing it with black coveralls he'd found in a locker. A little face black and a stevedore cap and he was ready for action.

"I don't like the look of this at all," Barbara said, giving her fork a rest. "What if you run into an army of those things?"

"Let him do it his way, my dear," Schmidt said. "It's what he does."

His words were followed by a long silence. A tear slipped from one eye and she put down her silverware. Without another word she pushed away from the table, squeezed past them, and headed for the forward stateroom.

"She'll be all right," Schmidt said.

"Sure she will," Carter said, not really convinced. He didn't need hysterics just before the kind of hard probe he was about to initiate. "No matter. I'm off. Black this place out until I'm out and in the clear."

Schmidt pulled the master switch and everything was pitch-black. Carter stood in the salon checking the location of his extra clips and slings of grenades. By the time he was satisfied, his night vision was good enough for an exit. He moved to the rail, lifted the camouflage, and became a part of the night.

No stars were visible. Thick clouds blanketed the sky making the night as dark as he'd seen it. The Killmaster stood still for a moment until he could see clearly, then picked out a trio of landmarks to point his way back to the camouflaged ship.

He could hear voices. He stood rigid and listened. Ten. No. More. A dozen at least.

Slowly, picking his way carefully, aware that he could not dislodge a single pebble, he moved to the highest crest of the small island. He could see lights below and to his right. He raised the sight of the rifle to his right eye and steadied it against a large boulder. Schmidt had provided a night scope. A half-dozen men were grouped together, not moving, probably talking strategy. He could see them as if it were midday.

A grenade would finish them off but it would alarm the others. But where had they gone? He moved the gunsight to the left and picked up a lone sentry. When he was sure the man was completely alone, he drew in a breath, squeezed the trigger gently, and felt the unfamiliar gun buck in his hands.

Quickly he found the target again. He was down, a hole the size of a quarter in his head. All right. That was the name of the game. He'd seen the room where the clones were put together and wondered idly if they had replaced some of the ones he'd destroyed. He doubted it. He and Barbara had been keeping them too busy.

He shook himself and cursed his lack of concentration. He'd seen too many good men go down for the same kind of lapses. All right. Where were the rest of them?

He found a sentry to his left and another about a hundred yards left again. He looked back to the first man, inhaled, and squeezed the rifle gently. The man was thrown against the rock in back of him, an involuntary grunt escaping his lips. Carter cursed silently. If he could hear it, they all could.

He quickly moved his weapon to the left again and found the second man looking toward the noise, raising his rifle, getting ready to investigate. Carter put a steel-jacketed slug through his chest and another through his head as he started to go down.

The M-14 was a wonder. He had it set on single shot but he could fire bursts if he chose. It had a recoil he could handle and it was accurate to within a hair's breadth. The noise of each shot was no more than a slight pop. The only negative factor was the smell of cordite that drifted on the night air.

The sound of leather against rock behind him drew his attention. He twisted to the right and down as a knife struck the rock next to him and came to rest at his feet.

The stalker had been too confident. Before he could move, Hugo was in Carter's right palm and the blade was finding space between the man's ribs. He died as Carter quietly lowered him to the rocky level.

Four down. He put the scope on the first group and found them still standing, trying to decide on their next move.

Perhaps he'd been wrong about the numbers. He scanned the rest of the island and came up with one more man, a solitary clone posted below and behind him.

He brought the M-14 to bear on the last sentry, squeezed off a shot, and heard him go down.

He waited and listened. The group below hadn't heard anything. Okay. He had to go after them and now. If they split up, the job would be twice as hard.

He moved as silently as a shadow. A rush of adrenaline had filled him with energy, had given increased sensitivity to every nerve in his body.

At fifty feet Carter stopped and looked over the rock in front of him. They were still there but the argument seemed to be concluded. They were reaching for the weapons they had laid aside and were preparing to go.

The Killmaster wished he'd had time to familiarize himself with the unique gun. But he'd fired an M-16 grenade launcher before. He loaded, raised the barrel, and pulled the trigger.

The noise of the launcher seemed twice as loud as he remembered. But it had been deathly still until then. He saw the faces of the clones and one security man turn up to him as the grenade exploded in their midst.

They were flung in all directions, all wounded. But Carter knew the small grenade had no real kick. He lobbed three more in the circle of downed men before a pain like a baseball bat against his skull turned everything purple and spiraling toward a vortex of black.

Carter fought for control. Only one thing could have caused the blow, an unseen enemy. He whirled to see a clone behind him, his rifle held like a club raised to descend on Carter's head again.

Hugo was out and in his hand in a reflex action. As the towering figure brought the gun down again, Carter countered with an upward thrust and skewered his assailant in the sternum. The big man turned on the knife and fell across Carter's legs. With his head still spinning, the man from AXE couldn't move.

He sat, vulnerable, the big man across his legs. Double vision turned the dark sky into hills and gullies of roiling black clouds. He concentrated with every ounce of energy he had and was rewarded when one clone came running from between the rocks just as he'd freed his arms. Carter shot him in the chest and watched him go down. He squeezed his legs from beneath the dead clone, tottered to his feet, and started to look for the landmarks that would lead him back to Schmidt's boat.

The way back was not easy. Carter's head throbbed and his memory was out of whack. Where the hell was the boat? He wasted precious time scouting the whole coast before he recognized the landmarks he'd picked out and reached for an edge of the camouflaged material.

He was bathed in light momentarily as he lifted the cloth and slipped under as quickly as possible. He'd just crawled over the thwarts of the boat, his eyes still unaccustomed to the light, when Barbara rushed toward him and threw her arms around his neck.

"Nick! We thought you were dead!" she exclaimed, holding on so tightly he could hardly breathe.

"She's overreacting," Schmidt said, coming up the gangway from the salon, a huge grin on his face. "I told her you could handle yourself. You always do."

Carter disentangled himself, poured a cup of coffee, and sat apart from them.

"Well?" Schmidt asked.

"All clear for now. They'll be sending a party to search for the missing, of course. Our worst enemy is time."

"They've got their hands full," Schmidt told him. "The experimental ship's almost within range. We'll have to make our play soon."

Carter was looking at Barbara. "I'm not sure we'll all be ready when the time comes," he said.

"What's that supposed to mean?" Schmidt asked.

"He's talking about me," Barbara said. "He thinks I've gone soft on him."

Carter just looked at her, waiting.

"So a woman can get emotional once in a while. That doesn't mean I can't do my job," she said, brushing her hair back and starting to pull on the hood of her wet suit.

"You're sure you can handle this?" he asked, his voice low but the concern unmistakable.

"The great Nick Carter doesn't understand women as much as I thought," she taunted. "Of course I can. My concern for your safety doesn't change my ability to do my job."

"What if I'm hit? Are you still going to do your job, or are you going to break off and come to me on the run?"

"We won't know that until it happens, will we?"

"That's not good enough," Carter said, trying to keep his tone strong enough without turning her off altogether. "If they hit you, I'd still have to complete the job we've got to do. I'd come back later to see if I could help, but the job comes first."

She maintained eye contact with him and didn't speak. Finally she nodded and continued to pull on her wet suit.

"Before I took off, you were saying not to worry about you, that you wouldn't be here," Carter said, turning to Schmidt.

"I've got to be able to see what's going on close to the action. Something like a forward observation post."

"And how do you propose to do that? I don't want you in the action," Carter said, shaking his head. "Keeping an eye on Barbara is enough. I don't want to find myself on the carpet at Dupont Circle trying to explain to Hawk how you died and why I let you get so close to danger."

"Come topside," Schmidt said, heading up the salon gangway to the forward deck and a cleared area ten feet square. He pulled a tarpaulin off a pile of galvanized piping and stood back.

"What is it?" Barbara asked.

"A helicopter," Schmidt said, already in the process of threading one hollow pipe into another. Within fifteen minutes he had assembled a lightweight frame complete with wheels. He levered the top off a small crate nearby and lifted out an alloy motor. It fitted beneath the rotor and was connected within minutes.

"I can stay in the air for three hours on one tank of gas. I'll use one of the rescue ships as a base for refueling if I have to. The radio I'll carry on this thing will be strong enough to signal you when Zendal makes his move and I'm ready to activate the announcement in the cavern. Do you really think the scientists will get out?" he asked.

"We'll have done all we can for them," Carter said. "The drugs should have worn off. They'll already be questioning why they are there."

"I think they'll move fast when they hear the announcement," Barbara added. "My concern is how long it'll take to unload two subs and get them underway. They might have to fight off some clones."

"You both worry too much," Carter said. They were back in the salon and he was starting to pull on his wet suit. "I don't think Zendal's got clones to spare now. Besides, I've seen what humans can do when faced with survival or death. We're talking about several hundred highly intelligent people here. It's up to them, right?"

"He's right, Howard. We've done all we can for them," Barbara said. "When do we go?"

"I've been monitoring Zendal's frequency for hours," Schmidt said, his eyes never leaving the woman. Even in a hooded wet suit her appearance was mesmerizing. "He's in his war room now and the ship is in his magnetic field. I think we should be in position as soon as possible."

"Okay. Let's do it," Carter growled.

Schmidt followed them to the stern launching hold. The sleds had been pulled inside and hosed down with fresh water. "I've held back one item about the sleds. You should know about it now," he said, looking very serious.

Carter sensed that something was worrying his old friend. Schmidt was about to reveal something that gave him pangs of conscience. He'd never seen him like this. "What is it, Howard?" he asked gently.

Schmidt didn't answer right away. He unscrewed four oversize butterfly nuts from the left half of one of the sleds and the whole cylinder, motor and all, came away as a separate piece.

"What is it?" Barbara asked. "It looks like a small torpedo."

"Nuclear," Carter said. "It's nuclear, isn't it, Howard? That's what's bothering you."

"You turn the cone at the front a half degree to charge it and set the course on this dial," Schmidt said, ignoring the question.

"You've always felt the military took advantage of science in the use of nuclear power, right?" Carter asked.

Schmidt didn't answer. The truth was evident on his face.

"We don't have time for a debate," Carter said. "We'll talk about it when this is over."

Barbara Wall moved to the grizzled middle-aged scientist and kissed his cheek. "I understand, Howard. And the decision is never easy. The torpedoes could stop Zendal from killing millions to get what he wants. Life's a trade-off sometimes."

"The other side of the sled will still take you out of the action when and if you use the torpedoes. Not as fast, of course, but they're a lot faster than swimming," Schmidt said, avoiding the concern of his friends. "Don't go to the booster when you're using only half of the sled."

Carter shook his hand for the first time that he could remember. Howard Schmidt had always been special to him but never more than now. Barbara hugged him. Then they pulled the sleds into deep water and disappeared beneath the surface.

TWELVE

Dr. Barbara Wall held on to the back rail of her sled and looked across at the man ten feet to her left. His sled was parallel to hers as they headed for the back side of Zendal's island.

Her mind wandered from the job at hand as she glanced at Carter, thinking about their time together and what they had done and were about to do. Her thoughts were a jumble. What had happened to the confirmed pacifist? She'd studied the martial arts purely as a defense against the hoodlums in the streets back home. But she'd seen men—or whatever the creatures were—torn to shreds and end up as shark food. She'd shot men herself, some in great haste, not knowing whether they were Zendal's clones or actual human beings.

Now she was going into battle. Her mind tried to conjure up images of the action to come, but she had too little background to make it work. The new navy ship would be gutted. Hundreds of sailors would be awash in angry seas. Some might die never knowing why. In the fantasy that was growing in her confused brain she saw hundreds of Zendal's men equipped with scuba gear, all intent on taking the nuclear weapons from the ship.

What would Admiral Brenner be doing? She'd been astounded at his response to Carter's warning. Absorbed within the confines of her academic environment, she hadn't realized that politics decided the course of their defense, first within the halls of Congress, then at the whim of senior officers. She'd never be as naïve again.

Howard Schmidt would be in the air now and she willed a silent prayer that he remain safe.

The sled that towed her was itself a deadly weapon. In her wildest dreams she could never imagine that she'd be this close to an atomic bomb, and worse, that she might be the instrument that would send it on its way.

Carter signaled for her to turn to the left. They were coming up on the island. When they rounded the southern tip of the huge hunk of rock, her fantasies would become realities and she wasn't sure she was ready for what that might mean.

Barbara Wall had never been a religious woman. Logic had dictated that beliefs were for those who had no core of strength within on which to build. But as her time neared, the time when she would know if she would live or die, the answers were not as pat. She was too alone, too hollow to face the battle without faith. So her last thoughts as they rounded the tip of the island were turned inward in a silent prayer for herself and for the man with her.

Carter's every sense, every nerve ending, was focused on the sight before him. The keel of the navy ship was a blur at the far limit of their vision, even in these crystal-clear waters. Scores of men were grouped at a staging point onshore. All they could see of them were their lower torsos and legs in the water, all encased in light blue wet suits.

"We'll surface carefully. I want to get a look at the action above," he said to Barbara.

"When you're ready."

He pushed forward and down on the control rod and the sled moved from the three fathoms at which they'd been traveling to break the surface with minimum wash.

"Neutralize your props," he ordered as he performed the act himself.

They bobbed in a three-foot chop about three hundred yards offshore. The navy ship loomed in front of them. "The ship's commander will have warned Brenner by now. We'll be seeing jets come in for a look-see fairly soon," he predicted. "I'd say we're going to see some action in the next few minutes."

"Schmidt calling N3. Come in, Nick."

"Loud and clear, Howard. We're on the surface. Looks like the stage is set."

"I've alerted Brenner. Apparently he'd heard moments before my call."

"He's sending observers first?" Carter asked.

"Right. I told him to warn his people about my chopper and about your sleds."

"Does Zendal have any sleds that you can see?" Barbara asked.

"No. All I see is a group of divers bunched at his main staging area. Dressed in light blue."

"We've seen them."

"Can't we do something for the navy ship?" Barbara asked as the three of them looked at the sleek craft from different vantage points. "It seems such a waste."

"We've covered that," Carter said. "Zendal's got to be totally preoccupied with the action to permit his captives to escape. Howard activates the announcements within the cavern as soon as the laser fireworks start."

"I can see you now," Schmidt said. "The navy jets should be able to identify you easily enough."

"Don't bet on it. I plan to be underwater for most of the action," Carter said. "How much time do you figure we've got?"

"Twenty, maybe thirty minutes," Schmidt answered, his craft now directly overhead.

"Two things," Carter said. "Radio the captain of the navy ship to have his belowdecks areas cleared. I'm going to do a deep dive to see what the bottom is like here."

"I'm with you," Barbara said.

"No. I want you to stand off the southern tip, submerged a couple of fathoms. If the action starts before I get back, I want you as my eyes up here."

He brought the props to full revs and started into the darker depths of the sea. Powerful spotlights helped him see for fifty or more feet ahead as he moved through the first two hundred feet. For the last two hundred, the range was cut to half that. He was on the bottom when his depth gauge showed four hundred and fifty feet.

Carter was directly below the ship. Directly in front of him, another hundred feet ahead, the *Sir Wilfred Laurier* lay on its side, a tear in its hull from bow to stern. She rested half on the shelf at four hundred and fifty feet and half over a deep drop that had to be several hundred feet deeper, perhaps thousands of feet.

He wondered if Zendal knew about the shelf. The man would have to be stupid not to know, and Zendal was not stupid. So the madman had pulled the ship in close with his magnetic field and she'd go down not far from the Canadian ship and well short of the deep.

He thought of the coming battle. His job and Barbara's would be to destroy the swimming teams of clones either before they got to the bombs or as soon after as possible.

An idea formed in his mind and he tucked it away for future use. He'd seen enough for now. He couldn't afford to have the action start without him, so he started for the surface as fast as he could without using the boosters. There was no way he wanted the bends again. Even the mild case he'd had brought with it excruciating pain.

When he reached the surface, he found Barbara where he'd told her to post herself.

"Any change?" he asked her as he closed to twenty feet of her sled.

"The divers have gone under. They're spread out in teams in front of the landing area."

"Teams? Makes sense. How many?"

"Looks like seven. Six men to a team."

"Seven teams. Six nuclear missiles. One spare team."

"What did you see below?" she asked.

He told her about the shelf a hundred feet past the navy ship, but he didn't mention the broken hulk of the Canadian ship on the bottom. He felt she didn't need that right now.

"So we destroy the seven teams before they get to the ship?" she asked. She knew they'd already gone over the plan, but he might want to change it based on his recon of the sea floor.

He told her of his new plan and she agreed.

They were two fathoms down and about five hundred yards from the enemy staging area.

"They've gone," she said, alarmed.

"Gone? Where?" Carter asked himself as much as she.

"They can't have moved toward the ship. They'd be pulled down with her and out of control," she offered.

"So the only answer is down," he said. "I'm going to warn Howard. Stay put," he ordered.

On the surface he didn't waste time. "N3 to Schmidt. Come in."

"What is it?"

"The divers have taken up positions in the deep. We're going to look for them," he reported.

"So we're only seconds away from zero hour," Schmidt said. "We'd better find those bastards before they disappear altogether. How many are—"

Before he could finish the sentence a beam of amber light cut through the air between the rock and the ship. The whole operation had happened so fast that neither man had time to react. By the time Schmidt tripped the radio-controlled announcements, the ship was torn from bow to stern at the waterline and was already heeling over to port.

Carter dived to join Barbara. "It's started," he told her. "We'd better find the teams before the sea gets too muddied up."

With Carter leading they circled the crippled ship, keeping far enough away to keep the whole scene in front of them. No divers could be seen, but as the U.S.S. *Lance* took on more and more water, they could see man after man hit the water and rise slowly back to the surface. The sea was covered with life preservers, rafts, and debris long before she went down.

The pair maneuvered their sleds in ever-deeper circles beneath the stricken ship, but they saw no one.

Schmidt checked his gauge and found his fuel was down to less than an hour of flying time. Already he'd seen enough for a lifetime of field work and asked himself why he wanted to get into the thick of things like Carter and meet the enemy face to face. He'd seen the crippling of the ship. He'd seen her heel over more and more, observed seamen diving from the decks, some throwing objects over the side, others waiting for nothing before leaving the ship. They bobbed around the port side as others slid along the canted deck to be crushed against the rail, their bodies plucked free by swirling eddies as she went under.

It was a sad sight to watch. She rolled completely over, trapping some air in the hull, then slowly went down, stern first, while some of the survivors struggled to keep away from the downwash. Some didn't make it.

He'd warned the scientists inside the rock at the first sign of action. He wouldn't know if they were going to escape for some time yet. They'd have to clear their own way first and he had no idea of the resistance they'd meet.

At his altitude he could see the first of the navy jets screaming in on the scene and rescue ships sailing down on the horizon. They'd have to move fast if they were to minimize casualties.

He couldn't do anything where he was, so he headed for the first of the rescue ships to report what he knew and to refuel.

Throughout the huge cavern, the announcement blared:

Warning! This is an agent of the United States government speaking. You have been under the influence of mood-altering drugs. Your leader, the man you call His Excellency, is in the act of sinking a U.S. Navy ship to steal its nuclear missiles. He has to be stopped. Go to the sub pens and help unload the subs. Your only chance of escape is to make room on the subs for all. Warning: Most of your captors are out of the cavern in the action above, but some might have remained behind. Armed men dressed in light blue uniforms might try to stop you. If you do not overcome them, you will die in the cavern, if not now, then later. Zendal is insane. He is an extremely dan-

gerous man. You must escape! Leave now! Warning!
This is an agent of the United States . . .

Zendal sat in his control room. He saw the U.S.S.
Lance go down and the seamen floundering in the water.
Someone on his staff piped the announcement into the
control room. Zendal sat, stunned, listening to the drone of
the warning.

"Get me Schnieder!" he roared.

"He was killed during the search you ordered," one of
the security men answered.

"Where's his assistant?"

"Dead."

"What the hell . . ." he bellowed, his voice filling the
whole chamber. "Get down there and stop the evacuation!
How many of your soldiers are available?"

"Two. We've lost too many and you haven't replaced
them."

"Take them and hold the eggheads at the sub pens. If
they get away, you're a dead man."

The security man, a soldier of fortune who'd signed on
for promised loot, knew when his number was up. He
rushed to the guardroom where the two clones were waiting for orders. He took the weapon from one of them, slid
back the cocking lever, and emptied the clip on them,
leaving the smell of blood and cordite in the small room as
he headed for the scientist's quarters, a lab coat, and
freedom through the sub pens.

Visibility was cut to only a few feet as the ship settled
on the bottom. Men were still leaving the hull, slowly
drifting to the surface—life preservers tied awkwardly to
lifeless bodies—or drifted with the swirls and eddies created by the ship's descent.

Carter steeled himself to ignore the dead and concentrate on the divers. "Do you see any?" he asked Barbara.

"No."

"Let's keep going, and keep me in sight." Suddenly he pointed to their left. "Over there! One of the teams!" he said, swinging his sled to face the enemy. By the time he had the site lined up, they had disappeared and he wasn't about to make any guesses and hit possible survivors.

"We've got rescue boats overhead. Men are being picked up," Barbara told him.

"That's great, but keep your eyes down here."

She swung her sled to starboard a few degrees, then loosed a cluster bomb. Carter didn't catch up with the action until the bomb let go fifty feet in front of him, shredding a team of divers. They were in a pocket of clear water and Barbara had reacted perfectly.

"Nice shot," he said.

"Thanks," she said shakily. The words came over the intercom in a metallic tone but the fear could not be hidden.

"We've lost too much time. The teams might have slipped past us and taken the missiles already," Carter said, directing their tactics. "We'll swing around the wreck and try to pick them up from the other side."

"I'll take the port side."

He would have preferred to keep her in sight but knew she was right. If they went together, the enemy teams might circle the wreck on the other side and make it back to the rock.

"Keep me informed of everything you see. If you run into them, give me your position immediately."

"You can bet on that."

Nothing more was said as they swung off in opposite directions. The silt had already begun to clear, settling to the bottom, some of it spreading out and thinning as it moved away from the hulk. His lights cut through the murky water giving him almost a hundred feet of clear vision.

He could see the *Lance* clearly now. She was on her side, the superstructure pointing at him, the rip in her side out of sight on the other side.

Carter flipped the boosters on full and hung on as the sled pulled him through silt and past drifting bodies at forty knots. He rounded the stern and could see the beginning of the rip in her hull. It looked as if someone had taken a torch to her and she'd been made of butter. The power of the laser was unbelievable.

But he saw no one. No one alive. And no divers near the ripped hull.

He brought the sled to normal speed and headed for the opening. It was ten feet wide, an incredible tear, and he had no trouble maneuvering inside.

He found the bays that had held the missiles. The key word was "had." The missiles were gone.

"Carter to Wall. I'm in the *Lance*. The missiles are gone."

"I've just spotted them. Plan Sheep Dog in effect. I'm chasing them out to sea."

"Don't do anything crazy. I'll be with you as fast as I can."

"I'm two hundred feet off the bow, past it, running at a bearing of two-ten degrees."

"How many of them can you see?" he asked, going to full power.

"Two teams. They've got some kind of sling made of flotation material. They look like six pallbearers."

"Let's hope we can send them to hell!"

*   *   *

Barbara was dogging the two teams, chasing them further from their base and out over the deep as Carter had planned.

What were they doing? Splitting up. Logical. She wasted no time, pointing her sled at the one to port and firing a bomb at it. She pressed the wrong trigger and the bomb let go just twenty-five feet in front of her. The hundreds of deadly darts fanned out, slicing through the team as planned but only a fraction of them hitting their targets.

It didn't seem to matter. All six clones were hit and bleeding profusely. They loosed their hold on the missile and it plummeted out of sight.

The wounded figures thrashed about in the water creating a huge cloud of blood. A shark came out of nowhere, passing Barbara's sled as if she were standing still. In seconds it had one of the clones in its jaws, shaking it like a rag doll.

"What's happening?" Carter broke in on the horror that was enfolding in front of her.

"They split up. I had to take out one team. The place is full of sharks."

"Where's the other team?"

"Heading your way."

"Then get the hell out of there. Circle around the sharks to port and look for the other teams."

"Right. My idea exactly."

Carter was more than pleased with Barbara's performance. After all, she was a researcher and a scholar, not a trained agent who was used to this sort of action. If he could just get this finished and keep her in one piece he'd be satisfied, he said to himself. But his brain swung from thoughts of Barbara's safety back to the problem at hand as the team she'd spotted loomed in front of him.

They'd obviously seen what had happened to the other team. The two clones in the middle broke off and fired at him, their barbed spears missing by inches.

The others glanced over their shoulders and saw him coming on. Something deep inside their manufactured brains told them to bail out and they let go of the missile as if on a signal.

They were spreading out, swimming away from him as fast as they could.

Carter aimed his sled, swinging it to the center of the group, and pressed the trigger for a twenty-five-foot shot. Like Barbara's shot, many of the darts missed. But he had to have maximum coverage and enough hits to cripple every man. He didn't have to kill them. The missile had plunged to the depths of the ocean. All he had to do was take them out of action.

He left the six clones wounded and headed to port. He corrected for the bearing he expected Barbara to take. It would intersect a roundabout route the clones might be taking back to the island, or to some island they didn't know about.

"Two teams in sight." Her voice broke into his thoughts. "Bearing two-twenty-five a half mile southwest of the *Lance*."

"I'm on it. If you can get a clear shot, take it. If sharks show up, keep on the trail of the other team and keep me informed."

"Bomb set for fifty feet," Barbara said. "Oh, Jesus! I'll never get used to this. The sea's clear here. Got all of them, totally shredded. Oh, Nick, I think I'm going to be sick."

"Hang in there. If you throw up you'll choke on it. If you can't stop it, surface and get it over with."

"Bastard. You think it's a joke."

"No joke. Tell me where the other team is and get to the surface."

"I'm all right now. Really. I'm getting out of here. Sharks again. The other team's turned to starboard. You should be picking them up any minute."

Carter saw them from a distance. He could barely pick them up in his powerful lights. He thumbed the booster control and caught up to them in a hurry.

This group had seen too much defeat. They dropped the missile and turned on him in unison, firing their spears in a cluster.

Carter let the sled slow down. Spears clanged off the front of the sled, two bouncing off the nuclear warhead. While he knew it wouldn't blow until he primed it, goose bumps formed on his arms beneath the wet suit.

He fired. The clones were shredded, and the cloud of blood and mutilated flesh attracted the usual voracious shark pack.

"Where are you?" he asked.

"Did you get the other team?" she countered.

"Yes. I make that four missiles. Two to go."

"I'm a quarter mile to port of you. I can see your lights. I'll turn toward you. See my lights?"

"Got you."

"Your place or mine?" she asked.

"Got any ideas?"

"So the big chief needs ideas. Sure. I think the others are between us and shore."

"Then let's go. I'll keep to the south of you. We search all the water between here and the island."

Time passed slowly. They'd been in the water a long time. His arms were weary from hanging on to the sled for so long. He wondered how Barbara was making out. After fifteen minutes of silence he opened his mike again. "See anything?" he asked.

"Negative."

"How do you feel?"

"About the same as you. I'm tired and I'm pissed."

"We'll get them. Give it another half hour."

"They could be in snug harbor by now."

"No way! Hey! I've got one! Trying to sneak back from the southwest," Carter said as he turned his sled to face the enemy, his lights off.

He didn't wait for them to come to him. He fired the maximum-distance trigger and turned on his lights five seconds later. He was just in time to see the bomb discharge its barbed missiles. The team was stopped in its tracks, the missile dropped, the sea filled with the usual black cloud of blood and limbs.

Carter headed for the missile and followed its path downward, not sure they were out past the shelf. He needn't have worried. At five hundred feet it was still heading down into a black void. Five down and one to go.

Slowly he rose back to the surface, taking a good half hour. Barbara had called him twice and he'd explained he was on his way up and trying not to ascend too rapidly.

She met him as he broke the surface. Before they could communicate Schmidt broke in on them.

"Schmidt calling N3. Come in."

"N3 here, Howard. Talk to me."

"God Almighty! I've been trying to get you for almost an hour. Where the hell have you been?"

"Doing our job, Howard. Got five. Lost one."

"That's better than I expected. Don't worry about it. I've been doing some cruising and I'm pretty sure I know their launch sites," Schmidt said, his voice confident in the static of their imperfect transmission. "I've arranged a bunk for each of you on one of the rescue ships."

Carter looked at Barbara and she shook her head. He grinned at her and gave the thumbs-up sign. "We're not coming in until this is over, Howard. So you'd better show us where the launchers are."

"Don't be so goddamned stubborn. We don't have to hurry now. They can't possibly launch in less than twelve hours. Brenner can have raiding parties there in no time."

"No way, Howard. We don't want a madman on trial at the taxpayer's expense. We don't want a field day for the press. We finish it nice and clean."

"You call nuclear annihilation nice and clean?"

"We're not coming in until it's over. Clear the area if you can. We've got a place to rest for an hour or two. We'll call you when we're ready."

THIRTEEN

"What next?" Barbara asked. "What are we really going to do?"

"I'd like to be sure of our ground before we take a breather. Just how tired are you?"

"I've got my second wind. I'm curious about the whole scene. Why don't we take a look around?"

"My thoughts exactly. Let's start first with the sub pens. I'm concerned about the scientists. Since Zendal knows he's lost, he could be taking it out on them."

He didn't wait for an answer but turned the sled 180 degrees and headed for the island rock that was Zendal's headquarters.

The submarine pens were alive with activity. The two huge diesel subs had been off-loaded and the civilians were bunched up near the conning towers. They were hiding behind crates, running for the conning tower runways a few at a time. Bursts of small-arms fire pinned them down. While Carter and Barbara watched, their sleds secured at the entrance, a couple of women were cut down by a hail of bullets, their bodies falling into the water.

"Who's in charge here?" Carter demanded.

A group of men turned toward him, surprised that anyone had come at them from the entrance.

"I guess you could say that I am," one of the men said. He was tall and gaunt, too old for the job he'd undertaken. He looked as if he should be retired or sitting in a lab with his white mice and microscope. "I'm trying to get everyone on board, but we're under fire as you can see."

"Have you any weapons?" Carter asked.

"There's a gun cabinet in each of the subs, but I can't get to them. They're in what used to be the officers' ward room."

"My knife and gun are in the compartment of my sled," he whispered to Barbara. "Get them while I see what I can do here.

"How many men do they have?" he asked the civilian.

"I don't know. Gunfire is coming from three places." He pointed out the areas of fire and while he was in the process, one of them opened up, chipping way at the stone near where they stood.

"AK-47s," Carter said.

"How do you know?"

"The sound. Some guns have a distinctive sound. And I saw a flash of orange from one of them."

"What's that?"

"They have orange-colored plastic ammunition clips. They're shaped like bananas and they're almost the same color," Carter said. "Tell me about the gun rack inside. Do any of the SMGs have extra tubes on the bottom?"

"SMGs?"

"Submachine guns."

"I've seen one with an extra tube and what seems like an extra trigger guard."

"Where?"

"The sub farthest from us, unfortunately."

Barbara returned with his weapons wrapped in plastic while they spoke.

"You'd better take the Luger," Carter said. "Keep everyone under cover and give me cover fire. You've got a clip in the gun and one extra. When they fire on me, give them return fire. Conserve as much as you can."

He didn't wait for her confirmation. She'd proved she was capable of following orders and able to handle the gun.

Gaining access to the sub farthest away was a lot simpler than he'd expected. A rope ladder was hooked onto the starboard conning rail. It was out of the line of fire of the enemy. Still in his wet suit but with bare feet, Carter dived into the water of the huge sub pen and didn't emerge until he was directly below the ladder. He wasn't exposed until the last moment when he pulled himself over the cowl and crept to the slatted floor of the conning tower. They had only a fraction of a second to spot him and no time to react.

The sub was alive with those who had made it already. They were impatient to get away but were not about to leave without their friends.

"Where's the ward room?" Carter asked one of the men.

"Which one?"

"Officers."

"Follow me," the man said. He was younger than the man in charge outside, and in far better physical shape. It posed the question why the roles were not reversed, but Carter had more important things on his mind. "Are you looking for the guns?" the man asked.

"Right. Why haven't you broken them out?"

"What for? We don't know how to use them."

"You could . . ." Carter started, then decided against a

debate. He couldn't see how they could be under siege and not try to use anything and everything available, but then he couldn't put himself in their place.

"This is it."

The cabinet had been broken open and a semiautomatic rifle was lying on a table. Carter had seen one in a catalogue in Schmidt's basement information section. It was designated XM-15 and was equipped with a forty-round magazine. The cocking lever was jammed but released easily enough when he released the magazine and removed a round jammed in the breech.

The locker contained two rifles identical to the first and several extra magazines. He took only one, planning to use three-round bursts. If he couldn't clear them all out with eighty rounds, they were all in big trouble.

The gun cabinet yielded one pleasant surprise. He found no grenade launcher, but three fragmentation grenades were clipped to a web belt at the bottom of the cabinet. He strapped on the belt and shoved the extra clip of ammunition under it and was on his way out.

This time he wasn't going to swim back. He waited in the conning tower until he saw a muzzle flash and let go with a three-round burst. He was sure he hadn't hit anything, but the shock value permitted him to jump from the tower to the body of the sub and take up a position behind the tower.

When all three positions opened up on him, he let them waste their time and ammo bouncing shots off the thick steel plating, then gave them a burst from the rear of the tower followed by one from the front a few seconds later. In the lull that followed he was on the edge of the pen and crouched beside the civilian leader in seconds.

"How are they inside?" the older man asked.

"Impatient but in no danger." He turned to Barbara. "I

heard your cover fire. Thanks. We're going to have to do it again."

"What's the plan?"

He'd changed his mind about his tactics while he was fighting his way back to them. "Here, you take this gun. Put it on single shot and pop a round at them every time they try to poke out a head. I'll feel more comfortable with my own weapon anyway." He strapped on the Luger while they talked. With the web belt he'd found inside, the gun harness around his left shoulder and Hugo in his chamois sheath on his right forearm, he looked like a commando. The appearance wasn't deliberate but it didn't hurt to use every tool you could.

Without further instructions, the Killmaster moved off on feet cushioned with thick calluses, gliding from rock to rock, always out of the line of enemy fire.

One of the firing positions opened up on Barbara's position. While the sniper was occupied, Carter pulled the pin on one of the grenades and lobbed it overhand to the gun flash. It exploded with a fury that shook the rock foundation of the cavern and hurt the eardrums of anyone within a hundred yards.

While no noise came from the target area, Carter knew that he had hit his man. While he looked at the area from a vantage point he'd climbed to above the action, one of the other enemy snipers made a break for it and Barbara took him out with one shot to the shoulder and another to the chest as the clone spun and fell.

Two down. Did they have just one more to eliminate? He crept from one rocky outcropping to another at the lower end of the cavern until he spotted the last man. He was crouched behind a rock. On bare feet Carter was able to creep up on him and finish him with a quick slash across his throat from behind. He wiped the blood from Hugo and waved to Barbara.

"That was the last one," he shouted at her. "Get them all loaded and underway."

"Where are you going?"

"I'd like to know if Zendal's still here. If I can get him, it's all over."

"Okay, but please be careful. I'll be with the sleds when you get back."

Carter moved from rock to rock until he found the rugged path that led upward, and he snaked along it, his Luger in his hand, until he reached the labyrinth of corridors of partitions that separated all the living quarters and working spaces between the pens and the upper part of the cavern.

He could imagine eyes on his back as he literally flew along the corridors on his way to the control room and the madman who had started this entire nightmare. Any door could hold an enemy but he didn't think they would. Zendal would have damned few men left with him, Carter figured. Between Barbara and himself they had disposed of almost a hundred clones and a half-dozen security men.

The body count hadn't occurred to him until he had to figure the odds. He wasn't a mass killer. He'd killed often enough under orders and was authorized to kill when absolutely necessary during an important project. His designation N3 indicated his lofty status in the intelligence community. But to kill a hundred men, even creatures designed for killing, didn't sit well with him.

It couldn't be helped, he rationalized. Before this was over, he'd most probably kill again.

As the thought occupied part of his brain, he was still alert for any sign that he was not alone. The communications control room high up on the cavern wall was in darkness. Zendal's headquarters room was lighted but empty. He saw no one.

They had to be somewhere, Carter knew. Was it possible that they'd escaped to another island nearby? Schmidt said he'd seen a couple of possible launch sites. Zendal was probably at one of those.

While he searched the upper level where Zendal had ruled supreme, he noted a large steel door in the far wall of rock. He ran to it, unclipped a grenade, and ripped out the pin. He left the grenade at the base of the door at one corner and dived behind a stack of crated equipment for cover.

The blast tore at his eardrums. When the dust and rubble cleared, Carter strode out to examine the damage. He could find none. The grenade had blasted a lot of rock from one corner of the door but the steel wasn't even scratched.

So much for that, Carter grumbled to himself. Zendal was either behind the door or at one other location that Schmidt had spotted. They'd have to get at the madman some other way.

Waiting had never been one of Barbara Wall's strong suits. She'd waited while Carter entered the sub, taking the occasional potshot at the enemy. She'd covered for him while he snaked among the rocks and destroyed two of the three enemy positions. And she'd been shaken to her very soul when she'd heard the distant explosion that meant he'd encountered opposition in the upper reaches of the cavern.

When she finally saw him emerge from the trail above, tears of relief filled her eyes. The subs were full and the diesel engines throbbed as the men brought them up to full revs in a test check.

Slowly the first sub moved out and the second began to leave its mooring. As its conning tower passed her, a lone figure on the cement sub pen docking, three men and a woman in the conning tower waved.

She felt an arm around her shoulder and she rested her head against him as they waved back together.

The sub slipped out into the night leaving the cavern a hollow and empty place.

"What was the explosion?" she asked.

"There's no one left up there. A huge steel door might lead to another part of the cavern. Zendal might be in it setting up the missile."

"So this place has to go."

"Right."

"Too bad. It could have some archaeological significance."

"You'll find evidence in other caverns."

He took her hand and led her to the sleds. He tossed the XM-15 in the water and the web belt followed. He wrapped his personal weapons in plastic and stowed them again. "Come on," he said. "Let's get back to the surface."

They were barely out of the sub pens when Schmidt called.

"Schmidt to N3. Come in." His voice sounded impatient, as if he'd been calling for hours.

"N3, here. We were checking on the subs."

"I saw them leave. Any trouble?"

"Some. Nothing we couldn't handle. What's your progress?"

"I got it all sewed up. There are two launch sites. One is at the other end of this piece of rock."

"It figures," Carter said.

"The other is about twenty miles away, the fifth island southwest in this chain."

"You're sure it's the fifth?" Carter asked.

"Positive."

"All right," Carter said, thinking about the island where he and Barbara had met. It was the third island in that particular chain. "We're going to take that rest we've been promising ourselves."

"Uh, I'm not so sure that's such a good idea right now."

"Why?"

"Brenner's mounting an attack force."

"Shit! Goddamn that man!" Carter snarled in frustration. "You tell him that he's got to pull his force at least ten miles from here. If he doesn't, he'll lose more of his precious ships."

"I don't think he'll listen."

"You pull all the rank you can, right up to the president. Tell him we'll reveal his weakness if he's stubborn. The secretary of the navy'd be quite interested in his action ignoring a positive threat from a reliable source," Carter went on, totally disgusted with the actions of Brenner. "Isn't the secretary a friend of Hawk's?"

"Yes. I'll tell him."

"Okay. We'll attack in four hours," Carter told him.

"It's a quarter of four. Why not say eight in the morning? We don't want to cut it too fine."

"Eight it is. Be sure to get Brenner and his people out of here."

"What about you two? You'll be caught in the tidal wave."

"That's a possibility. We'll shelter behind the farthest island we can get to. Over and out."

"Wait a minute. I wanted to tell—" But the connection was broken. All the big man could see in his helicopter was the two sleds planing downward as they sought the privacy that the deep would give them.

"I'd like to see a few things before we head for the island," Carter said to Barbara when they were well out of sight.

"Like what?"

"Have all the survivors been picked up? The *Lance* is on the bottom. The silt should have cleared by now."

"Lead on."

They'd covered most of the distance from the island to the area of the sinking before he spoke again. "Are you sure you want to see your ship?"

"I'm over it, Nick. I might as well take a good look while I'm here. I might have to talk to relatives."

The rescue operation was completed. Every sailor still living had been pulled from the water. Carter was sure the navy men would have tried for the bodies of the dead, but the ones they didn't get would have been eaten by sharks by now. Not one piece of the ship or its survivors was evident in the water around the armada of ships bobbing in the six-foot chop.

"I'm going down," he called to Barbara.

The two sleds moved in unison to a depth of 450 feet. The two ships lay within a hundred feet of each other. Carter examined the American naval vessel while Barbara circled the *Sir Wilfred Laurier* before returning to him.

"Do you want to take anything off it?" he asked.

"No. Anything I want they'll get for me when they salvage her."

"Don't be too sure."

"What do you mean?"

"The ships are close to the drop-off. Our final act could cause enough backwash to push them over."

"Oh, no!" She held her sled in the water for a long moment before she turned its nose to their island haven.

He moved ahead and took the lead. They'd have to rise to the surface slowly to avoid bubbles of nitrogen forming in their blood. As they held on and the sleds pulled them further from the scene, he thought about the "minor incident" he'd been asked to investigate and smiled to himself. Who would have believed that mad scientists still existed? Who could believe that he could con so many to help him, malcontents or not?

There seemed to be an inexhaustible supply of evil in this world. But then, if everything were roses and caviar, there wouldn't be a need for organizations like AXE. He looked at the woman who had pulled alongside him. In a perfect world he could spend his time on tropical islands with a bright, gutsy, gorgeous woman like Barbara Wall and never be a slave to a phone call from Washington. Carter sighed. He could get very used to a world like that. . . .

FOURTEEN

Carter had a fire going in the shelter of their cove. They'd come to think of it as "their island," a haven where they'd discovered each other and bonded their friendship.

But neither thought of the physical part of their relationship at that moment. The day had given way to night and the sea breeze was warm. It washed their skin while it dried out their wet suits and the thin cotton long johns they'd worn underneath. Again they were unclothed, sitting by the fire, preferring to be one with nature rather than lounging in the luxury of the Chriscraft that still sat in the bay nearby.

Carter had fish cooking beneath the fire as Kuhuhu had just a few days earlier. They lay back, waiting for it to be done, their hands behind their heads, their eyes on a sky that was filled with suns of other galaxies.

"I can't believe I've been a part of this," Barbara said, turning toward him, her breast nestling in the soft sand. "I've always been a pacifist. Even when taking karate, all the months of practice and instruction, I cringed inside every time I tossed an opponent or hit someone accidentally."

"You don't have to go through this, you know. It's all but over."

"I've got to see it through to the end. That's just the way I am."

"So I've noticed. You're a very special lady. I'm going to miss you."

She turned back and looked up at the sky. "Don't you ever take time off? You could call."

"And I will. My short vacations are always unscheduled, sometimes months apart."

"And I'll be off on a dig somewhere or caving on some remote Pacific isle."

"Why not take what we can now? I don't mean now, this minute—we've got to get some rest—but when we've dealt with Zendal once and for all."

"Why not? We could come back here, find our own food, sleep under the stars, make love . . ."

What he'd had in mind was a few days on Maui or maybe the big island. He knew of a few secluded guest houses off the tourist route. This place could be a shambles after the last part of the show. If Schmidt's nuclear devices were powerful enough to pulverize islands just ten miles from here, this place could be a wasteland. But he wasn't about to disillusion her. They'd come back here and they'd make it work if they could.

He looked at her, took in the beauty of her from head to toe before he closed his eyes. "We've got an hour before our meal's ready. I'll wake you then."

He closed his eyes and set his mental alarm for an hour, then drifted off to sleep before his tired brain could absorb another thought.

She awakened first and checked her watch before waking him. Six o'clock and still dark. It was just fifty minutes since they'd dozed off. She eased his arm from her chest and stepped over him on her way to the tidal pool. The water was warm against her skin. She was wide awake and refreshed when she walked up the beach to him, a shining goddess from the deep, her skin wet, her hair plastered to her shoulders, her figure perfect in the light of the stars.

Carter had been awake for a few minutes and he'd been watching her. He marveled at the easy rapport they'd achieved in so short a time, their ability to build up energy and not feel the need to spend it on a bonding of their bodies. That would come later. He was still concerned about her. He thought about it as he scooped away the hot coals and laid out their meal on large flat leaves. The last act of this battle seemed simple enough, but he couldn't be sure Zendal didn't have a second line of defense. He couldn't even be sure that the billions of dollars of naval power floating just a few miles away might blow the deal and give them trouble.

As she neared, he put it out of his mind, and when she sat with him they ate in silence, looking out at the Pacific, the moon peeking from a patch of cloud cover, turning the water to molten gold, flowing rivers of golden lava wafted across the nature's stage by a light chop.

When they were finished they lay back, each with one of his cigarettes, each with private thoughts. It was like the eve of battle, the warriors pensive, all too aware of what had gone on before and what they had to lose, but unsure of what fate had in store.

They seemed attuned to each other, moving in unison, deciding when it was time to go, burying the butts of their cigarettes, pulling on their dried clothing, stretching the rubber of their wet suits until they were comfortable. They didn't speak one word until they were at the water's edge and prepared to activate their sleds.

"We'll check in with Howard and make sure of our targets. Have you ever seen films of the early atomic explosions?" he asked. "The tests at Bikini?"

"A long time ago."

"They kick up one hell of a wave. When we fire our torpedoes, we'll be standing off about a mile. We turn a full hundred and eighty degrees and go to full power, booster power. I'm not even sure we'll be able to get clear."

"We meet back here? You promise?"

It was the last thing she asked before she put on her mask. He looked at the gold-flecked hazel eyes, now close to tears, and nodded. "We meet back here."

Carter started his sled and led the way back toward Schmidt and the fleet. Halfway there he called his old friend on their open line. "N3 to Schmidt. You read me?"

"Loud and clear."

"Where are you?"

"On one of Brenner's cruisers. I'll be up in a few minutes. I'm using one of his gunships. It's a little more substantial than my bundle of galvanized pipe."

While they talked, an F-15 came out of nowhere and strafed Barbara's position. The strings of lethal 50mm slugs missed her by inches.

"Howard! *Brenner's damned fool pilots are strafing us!* Get them the hell out of here! *Get the whole fleet the hell out of here!* Jesus Christ! The F-15's coming back for another pass. I'm diving. I'll call you in fifteen minutes!"

He tuned out and put the sled in a sharp dive as cannonfire from the jet ate up the water overhead. "Are you all right?" he asked Barbara.

"Yes. Was that one of ours?"

"Sorry to say, it was."

"What the hell's going on, Nick?"

He didn't know exactly how to explain. How did you describe to a civilian that mistakes were commonplace in warfare, that people got nervous and shot up everything that moved? "Someone goofed. It happens," he said. "Howard's going to fix it."

On the deck of Brenner's flagship, Schmidt strode to the admiral's headquarters and pulled the door open so hard it smashed against the bulkhead. If the glass window hadn't been shatterproof, it would have been in countless pieces all over the deck.

"What the hell is this?" Brenner demanded.

"I'll tell you what this is, you asshole. Your jets are strafing my people. I told you to get them out of the air. Now I'm telling you to get the whole damned fleet out of my way."

The senior officers present had never heard anyone talk to their CO like that. They waited for the explosion that was bound to come. The poor bastard was going to feel Cube Brenner's wrath.

Brenner didn't speak. Schmidt was too quick for him. "I can take this all the way to the president. You'll be finished. I told you to stay out of it and you had to play your fucking power games. *Now get the hell out of these waters!*"

"These are *my* waters!" Brenner shot back, but he was talking to empty air. Schmidt was out and on his way to his rendezvous.

In the air, Schmidt tried to reach Carter. Apparently his friend wasn't ready to surface. "Circle this area until we can make contact," Schmidt told the pilot. His heart was still racing. He was so furious with Admiral Brenner that he could barely think straight.

"N3 to Schmidt," Carter came through at last. "You get it fixed, old buddy?"

"Partly. The jets are out of our hair but Brenner's not about to budge. He's going to look like a prize fool when this is all over."

"Forget it. We've got work to do," Carter said. "You're sure it's the fifth island?"

"The first and the fifth. I've scouted both and can't be sure where he's got the stolen missile stashed."

"All right. It's got to be both of them for us. Keep clear, Howard. And try to get Brenner to move his people."

"No use, Nick. He's like a mule."

"Barbara's going to take Zendal's headquarters, the first island," Carter said. "Keep an eye open for her after the blast."

"I'll be in the air as soon after as I can. There's no way I can be airborne until it's all over."

"Do the best you can."

"Are you coming back to the fleet when it's over?" Schmidt asked.

"We'll call you. But we won't be back right away."

"Good luck, Nick."

The silence settled around them like a shroud as Schmidt's voice faded. The enormity of what they were about to do was almost overwhelming.

"You want me to take the headquarters," she said, finally breaking the silence.

"Yes. Do you remember how to detach and fire the torpedo?" he asked.

"Yes. Are you sure we're going to get a direct hit at a mile? It seems to me it'll wander off course."

"It's a magnetic seeker missile. There's enough metal

in the caverns to keep it on course and nothing to divert it."

"That's it, then. Be careful, Nick."

"You, too. You're sure you still—"

"I'm sure," she interrupted. "Let's do it."

"Okay. I hate to sound like an old war movie, but we'd better synchronize our watches. Fire at the same time. If we're going to have two nuclear explosions, I'd rather try to survive one. It's eight minutes past eight. We both fire at nine exactly."

"Will that give you enough time to get in position?"

"Plenty. See you at our island," he said, cutting out and turning to the southwest and his target.

When he'd gone, she felt more alone than she had at any time in her entire life.

Strangely, she didn't think of her own safety. But she was wasting time with gloomy thoughts. She checked her watch. It was half past the hour already. She wasn't in position and she wanted some time to check out Schmidt's instructions.

Ten minutes later she was in position, or as close to it as she could figure without instruments to give her exact distances.

It took her ten minutes to dismantle the missile from the sled and go over the instructions Schmidt had given them both. What about speed? They hadn't talked about speed. The missile had its own booster speed. Did Carter want normal speed at full revs or booster speed?

"Wall calling Carter. Are you in range?"

He came back at her faintly.

"The missile has booster speed. What do you want?" she asked.

"Set it at normal operation, full revs," he replied, his voice faint through the static.

"So that's no booster."

"Confirmed."

"We're guessing at distances, Nick. I'm usually able to guess distances well enough, but at water level I'm not sure."

"Do your best. It's not going to be exact. Just get the hell out when you've fired."

"Okay. I'm ready. Five minutes to go."

"Confirmed. Over and out."

She found it difficult to hold on to the missile with one hand and guide the sled with the other. Two minutes to go. When she was ready to fire, she would let go of the sled and pick it up when the missile was on its way.

The island seemed to loom up at her, mountainous and forbidding. She was sure she was about a mile away but it seemed so close.

Fifteen seconds to nine. She activated the primer of the bomb, pointed the missile at the middle of the island, and pulled the throttle all the way back.

The missile took off like a scared rabbit. She let go immediately, but she'd traveled fifty feet by the time she'd been sure the missile was on course. She churned back through the water to the sled, found it in ten fathoms, pointed it in what she thought was the opposite direction to the island, and yanked on the booster control.

The time was down to two minutes and slipping by fast. Carter was ready. All he had to do was arm the missile and let her go.

A spear flashed through the water near his head and another glanced off the missile. He turned to find a half-dozen clones in scuba gear less than twenty feet from him.

One minute to firing. He'd never turned from a fight, but this was no time for a challenge. He clung to the missile with his right arm and maneuvered away from the clones with the sled at half power.

When he was two hundred feet from them he turned, aimed the missile at the island, and let it go. It passed the clones on a direct track for the island. For a second or two he thought the missile might zero in on the metal of their tanks and they'd all go up together, but it headed straight and true for the island. It was a quarter of the way there before he turned the sled and left the scene on full booster.

FIFTEEN

The deep bass voice boomed out of the control room:
"Get the damned thing set up! The fleet out there could
send in a landing party at any minute!" Zendal screamed
at the few scientists who'd been with him while the others
escaped. "If I can't make my phone call to the president
soon, we could lose. You hear, you jackasses? We could
lose!"

The men in lab coats moved with all the speed of a
group of racing turtles as they prepared the missile for
firing. They hadn't had his mood-altering drugs for almost
two days and they knew now what kind of role they were
playing. It was "work to rule" all the way for them, or as
little as they could get away with.

The eyes that had once seemed wise and hypnotic now
seemed crazed and reptilian. Zendal was a madman, a
monster. If it wasn't for the half-dozen heavily armed
clones in the room, the civilians would have been on him
like a swarm of hornets.

Barbara felt as if she'd been holding on to the careening
sled for only a matter of seconds after firing her torpedo
before she felt the world erupt around her. She was thirty

feet underwater, but the concussion that ran through the sea from the incredible force that disintegrated the island pushed outward in every direction, from the depths of the ocean to a height of several hundred feet above the surface.

She knew she was going to die. It would all be over soon and she had never prepared for it. Young people didn't think they were going to die. Life was going to go on forever, or at least for one hell of a long time. Thoughts on death just weren't part of this healthy young woman—until now.

The force took her and her sled like a piece of seaweed, churned it to the surface, and carried it on the crest of a huge wave for what seemed like hours. She tumbled in the process so that she was looking at an unfriendly sky one moment and the green-black of an angry ocean the next.

At one point, above the crest of the wave—her arms almost pulled out of their sockets as she hung on desperately—she thought she saw the wave pick up a group of ships as if they were toys in a child's bathtub and toss them along as it was tossing her.

Howard Schmidt saw the incredible explosion of the first island and was glad he'd worn the dark glasses he'd brought along. Men beside him in Brenner's control room turned away and moaned as the bright new sun attacked them from less than ten miles.

Brenner stood beside him, he too wearing glasses to protect against the flash. "Jee-sus," the admiral breathed. "I've seen this on film, but it's . . . I can't describe . . ." He obviously couldn't go on.

"Look at the tidal wave form," Schmidt said. "It'll be several hundred feet high when it hits us."

"No way. That's impossible," Brenner said.

"Where's the nearest bedroom?" Schmidt asked.

"My quarters. The door behind you. Why?"

"I advise you to get your men rolled up in mattresses or something," Schmidt said.

"Nonsense. Don't be such an alarmist," Brenner replied. "My men and I will stand watch until this is over."

The second island went up like the first, and while it was almost twenty miles farther away, the flash was spectacular.

"Two separate tidal waves. Damn! I'd hoped they would be simultaneous—maybe cancel each other out."

"Get the hell out of my control room!" Brenner barked.

"My pleasure," Schmidt said as he headed for the stateroom.

It was large and more luxurious than he'd expected. He pulled the mattress off the bed, folded it in two with difficulty, and tied a sheet around each end to hold it closed like a hinged sandwich. He squeezed himself inside, the meat of the sandwich, and curled himself into a ball.

Zendal stood in his control room, his deep voice hoarse from screaming, his back to the window that looked out to sea.

A bright light illuminated the room for a moment, hurting his eyes. The two scientists standing in front of him started to change from white-coated apparitions to brown. In slow motion they seemed to blister and disintegrate until they turned to ash in front of him and blew away with the rest of the room.

His reaction was anger and disbelief, but the thought was only momentary because he too was dead and he was experiencing the last impressions of disintegration as his eyes and body transported the impression to a brain that was no longer there. He wanted to go on but

*   *   *

Carter had lost time in getting his torpedo away. He knew it would reach its target, but Barbara's would detonate first and they'd have two shock waves instead of one. As he clung to the sled that raced him from the destruction, he realized he'd be the only one to know. Barbara would feel the first, and have a good chance of surviving it, but she could be caught unawares by the second, off guard, vulnerable.

He tried to reach her through their underwater communications system. Static crackled through both sides of his headset and his voice was lost in the race to freedom.

The shock hit him in the middle of his concern for her and he was tumbling wildly, desperately holding on to the sled for what seemed like hours.

The pressure was coming from his left, from the north. It should have been right behind him. It dawned on a brain that was being tumbled about as if in a washing machine, that he'd been hit by Barbara's shock wave and not by his own.

The thought was barely born when he was picked up from the depths by a force from behind, carried to the surface, and planed on a wave, whose size even the most fanatical surfer could not imagine. He could see for miles. The sled performed perfectly, taking him straight ahead, a ride that lasted long enough to be ten miles or more.

Finally the force started to wane and he found himself sliding down the following trough. It seemed as low as the crest was high. The sled slipped to the bottom and kept on going, plunging to the ocean floor, taking him with it.

His mouth was raw from the power of the water that tried to dislodge his mouthpiece. He fought like a wounded tiger to keep the mouthpiece in, fought until his jaw muscles ached and finally cramped.

The pressure slowed. He had dived deep, possibly too deep. Slowly he started the long climb back to the surface.

Admiral Brenner stood with his men as the wave came at them. It was a wall as high as the tallest skyscraper and solid, boiling straight at them, stretching from horizon to horizon.

"Oh, shit!" his executive officer, a captain, said as he stood beside him. "The ship wasn't built for this."

"*Hang on!*" the admiral called out, but the wave had hit and the men were tossed from one bulkhead to another as the ship tumbled crosswise to the monster wave.

Barbara came to the surface and took the mouthpiece from her mouth as the huge wave left her in a relatively tranquil sea. She took a deep breath of fresh air, then realized it could be contaminated. What the hell. It didn't matter. She was either going to die or live. It wasn't up to her. Life had taught her a major lesson in a very few minutes, a lesson that would be with her as long as she lived.

She put the mouthpiece back in place just as the second wave hit. It was much weaker than the first. She figured she had to be at least ten miles from the explosion and the cresting wave had spent much of its power by the time it hit her.

As the wave passed she found herself deep beneath the surface and came up to have a look around. She was disoriented. Where were the landmarks she'd expected to use? All she could see in the whole ocean was three peaks. The fleet should have been to her right but she saw no ships. The three peaks had to be the middle three islands. Both targets were gone, sheared off or disintegrated at sea level or below. Incredible amounts of rock tonnage had been pulverized and blown away into the wind that whipped around her head.

Where were they all? Where was Nick Carter? She floated on the surface, the sled's power turned off momentarily, and she began to cry.

Schmidt gave it another fifteen minutes. The second shock had passed. He'd been thrown around the room like the ball in a squash court and he felt as if every part of him would be black and blue. But he was still alive.

He peeked out one end of the mattress. The room was a shambles, the furniture pulled loose from its sea fastenings and splintered from repeated battering against the bulkhead walls. Miraculously, he stood on the decking and not the ceiling when he pulled himself out of his cocoon, so the ship was upright.

He was almost afraid to examine the rest of the ship and what lay outside, but he forced open the damaged door and stared at the carnage in the control room.

The bodies had been smashed against the walls. They were lying flat on the floor, limbs at strange angles, torsos jellylike, as if all bone structure had gone on strike.

Brenner's body was in the far corner, his neck at an impossible angle, his eyes glazed, his mouth awash with blood and saltwater. Schmidt knew he had to tell Hawk the truth about the man's pigheadedness but suspected the dead here would all be afforded heroes' funerals.

He walked to a shattered window and looked out at the islands. They had been reduced from five to three. He found a pair of binoculars, one eyepiece cracked, and scanned the three islands. They had been devastated. He wasn't surprised.

Wind howled through the broken glass of the control room, almost at gale force. It was southwesterly and would

carry the radiation toward the least populated part of the
Pacific. By the time it passed over other islands, it would
be at relatively safe levels. Even the remaining pieces of
rock here would be inhabitable, but he couldn't imagine
anyone even mildly interested in them now.

Carter reached the surface and felt no aftereffects beyond
a great weariness. He turned the sled at low speed toward
the center island and his promised rendezvous. He had
survived but he had no assurance that anyone else had. He
looked around for 360 degrees and saw nothing but the
three towers of desolate rock.

The sled pulled him on, his arms numb from the strain.
He wasn't in a hurry. He wasn't even sure that he could
make it at full speed.

He saw no fish. It might be days before wildlife came
back to this blighted spot. But he'd slowed earlier to take
his stiletto from the sled's waterproof compartment and
strap it on. This was not unlike the aftermath of nuclear
war. No one had experienced it, so no one knew what to
expect.

As the thought occurred, a spear pierced his calf and
emerged from the other side, blood seeping from its shaft
at both ends.

He looked around in disbelief to see a clone racing for
him at full speed, his spear gun discarded, a long knife in
his right hand.

It was too late for a cluster bomb. Carter couldn't
maneuver the sled fast enough for a shot. Where had the
damned thing come from? he wondered. He didn't need
this. He never ran from a fight, but he was exhausted and
this thing was only part human. It had some bionic parts.
It might even have an artificial heart for all he knew. At
any rate, it would have one hell of a lot more strength and
energy than he.

He let the sled start to sink slowly and flipped Hugo into his right hand. Given the same odds on dry land he'd have thrown the knife, but this was not dry land. It was a David and Goliath confrontation in seawater.

The clone came on, his flippers churning behind, a testament to his strength. The thought of using the booster had occurred to Carter, but the damned sled would probably pull his arms from his sockets at this point, he was so tired.

As the clone closed in, Carter saw the shark. The Killmaster knew he had to get this over with and get out of there as fast as possible.

The first pass was a draw. The clone's oversize knife slit Carter's wet suit at his right temple and his stiletto carved a long slit down the clone's right arm.

The giant-sized enemy switched the knife to his left hand and came back as fast as the first time. Carter wasn't about to be fancy about the kill. He gave the clone his torso to go for, pulled in his gut at the last minute, and slashed Hugo's long thin blade across the massive neck as the figure passed.

Now, as the cloud of blood obscured his vision, Carter had to think fast. His assailant was finished but the shark was king of these waters and he'd have to be dealt with. The Killmaster peeled a long strip of wet suit from the clone and pushed him in the direction of the shark. While the huge fish made its first pass at the clone, Carter broke the thin shaft of the spear, pulled out both ends, and bound the wound with the strip of rubber.

The sled had sunk about twenty feet. Tired arms or not, he retrieved the sled, turned it toward the island, and flipped on its booster power. He wanted no more encounters with either man or beast.

*   *   *

Barbara positioned herself facing the three islands and dived to have a last look at the ship that had brought her there. She cruised the ocean floor along the ridge long enough to realize that the ship was gone, that they were both gone. The force of the underwater currents set up by the explosions had sent them to the deep. She doubted if anyone would find them or even mount an expedition.

When she started for the surface at the end of her search pattern she was way off to the southwest. A disturbance in the water ahead of her brought her up sharp. She put the sled in neutral until she knew what it was.

"My God," she muttered into her face mask. Two sharks were fighting over a body. "Nick!" she screamed, then saw an arm that was far from human. A clone.

She flipped the booster control on full and hung on for her life as the sled took her far to the south.

The island was dead. Carter could find no other way to describe it. All the trees had been uprooted. Everything but the shortest grass and moss had been torn loose and blown away, leaving fresh scars against the lava rock of the island's base.

The Chriscraft was a mass of floating splinters rocking back and forth in the narrow harbor that had been its refuge. Carter moved below the floating wood in his scuba gear and gradually salvaged enough undamaged supplies to last a survivor for a week or more. He even found a couple of bottles of wine, a first aid kit, and miraculously, a can opener. Later, he found the earth station wedged between two rocks, the cone slightly bent but otherwise undamaged.

The beach was no place to set up shop to wait for Barbara. He worked on his leg for a few minutes, then went exploring. On the lee side of the island he found a cave fifty feet above the level of the wrecked ship. The floor was coated with matted palm fronds, old but dry. He moved all his supplies to the cave and started a fire.

He was ravenous but settled on some tuna eaten from the can with his stiletto. The earth station was easy to repair. He was on the air in minutes broadcasting to Schmidt or anyone he could reach.

"Schmidt here. Christ, Nick, I wasn't sure I'd be hearing from you."

"I'm all right. I'm in a cave on the middle island."

"You should be all right there. I figure the fallout went straight up, then floated southwest."

"Barbara's not here. Did you see her?"

"No. I'm in a bit of a mess here myself. Brenner is dead and a lot of his people are too."

"Shit. How many?"

"Fifty. Maybe more. Most of the men were smart enough to protect themselves from the shock wave."

"Are the civilians from Zendal's cavern all right?"

"Everyone. More than seven hundred of them. They headed straight for Hawaii in their subs long ago, all but a few. Four or five were trapped with Zendal."

"So we took the right odds."

"If Brenner hadn't been so stubborn, we'd have a better survival rate. We lost twenty-five from the new ship, the *Lance*."

"What about Brenner's ships?"

"We had ourselves some kind of crazy miracle. There was lots of damage, but they were all topside up when it was over."

"Thank God for that."

"What about Barbara? Do you think she made it?"

Carter couldn't answer for a long time. He'd carried the earth station with him to the highest peak of the rock and hadn't seen a sign of her.

"Wait," he said, a note of wonder in his voice. "Wait a goddamned minute! Something is coming out of the water at the beach. It's Barbara's sled! I'll call you later!"

He was off to the beach as fast as one bad and one good leg would take him. She was stretched out on the sand when he got there, unconscious but alive and unhurt. He carried her up the steep slope to the cave as if she weighed ten pounds.

He put her down on the soft bed of fronds in the cave and emptied a can of soup into a pot that he placed in the fire. He pulled off her cold suit and the sodden long johns. Her limbs were blue. He massaged life back into her and held her close until she opened those incredible hazel eyes and smiled at him.

"What are you doing in your clothes on our island?" she murmured weakly.

"Don't try to talk. You need your strength. We—"

"Take your damned clothes off," she said, trying to struggle up on one elbow. "I dreamed about this all the way back. It was all that drove me on," she pleaded, her voice hoarse. "I want the feel of you inside me."

He pulled off his wet suit and the still damp long johns underneath and lay beside her. He held her against his body, his mouth to her ear. "It will wait. You need to gain back some strength," he whispered in her ear.

"No. I need to feel close, as close as we can get. God, Nick, we're lucky to be alive."

He kissed her slowly, his tongue intertwining with hers. Her breath was hot, her skin becoming warmer. He kissed her neck and reached for the hard tips of her breasts that had been soft only seconds before.

As he entered her gently and settled down for a long and slow encounter, he felt her start to chuckle beneath him.

"What's so funny?" he asked.

"Don't look now, but the ceiling over our heads is a treasure of ancient drawings, the kind of thing I've been searching for all of my adult life."

"What do they look like?" he asked, his ardor cooled but it didn't matter at that moment. He was content simply to lie with her, unmoving.

"You'll never believe it. Erotic scenes like some I've seen in Thailand and Malaysia. At least ten positions." She started to laugh, her belly moving against his, the motion creating a minuscule churning between them that inflamed him again.

"It's better than those bedrooms in Vegas. You know— the ones with the mirrors on the ceilings?"

He could see the humor of it. But it wasn't conducive to the lovemaking they'd started. Now that he knew she was safe, what he really wanted to do was sleep. His passion eased again. They could make love all they wanted to in a few hours.

He raised himself from her slightly to look at the beautiful face, the breath coming slower, the eyes closed. She was asleep, a smile on her face.

From the crest where he'd left it, the earth station squawked into life. "Schmidt calling N3," he heard faintly. "Come in, N3. Urgent message from Hawk. Come in."

But the man from AXE was not about to respond. He eased himself off the sleeping body and lay beside it. He felt Barbara's heart beat against his chest. Her breath was warm in the hollow of his neck as she snuggled closer, murmuring incoherently.

This was as it should be. It was the whole world to him right now. The rest could wait.

DON'T MISS THE NEXT NEW NICK CARTER SPY THRILLER

ARMS OF VENGEANCE

By dawn they were past Saharanpur and driving steadily northeast into the foothills of the Lesser Himalayas with the great crest of the Himalayas proper in the distance. Each took turns driving on the almost empty road, avoiding ox carts and people carrying great loads on their backs, while the others slept.

"Rishikesh," Sait Raju had told them, "is where the training camp is, near a great temple of Vishnu. It is past Dehra Dun and Tehri, with great Nanda Deva to guard it."

They reached the city of Dehra Dun before noon and drove on over the rugged road toward Tehri as the fields became forests of evergreen oak turning slowly into pines and firs, and the road began to climb steadily. Now the distant peaks of the great divide of the Himalayas was clear, and the isolated peaks even closer, with Nanda Deva dominating all. A mile beyond Tehri, Carter studied the rearview mirror.

"We've got some company."

Lalita and Raju turned to look behind them. A four-

193

wheel military-type small truck was less than a quarter of a mile back. It was driving very fast for the rugged and twisting mountain road.

"I first saw it behind us long before Dehra Dun," Carter said. "Then at Tehri. It could be nothing, but it's been following us for a long time."

"We'd better find out," Lalita said.

"You think," Sait Raju said uneasily, "it is someone who is not friendly to us?"

"Our friends don't know we're out here," Lalita said. "Unless someone told them."

"I did not," Raju said.

Carter shook his head, and watched the mirror where the truck was gaining on them. It drove wildly and dangerously on the narrow, winding forest road.

"And I didn't," Lalita said. She stared back at the small truck drawing nearer every moment. "It isn't any Indian army vehicle. It has no markings."

"But . . . but . . ." Sait Raju stammered. "I'm sure I see guns."

There was no mistaking the gun barrels protruding from both sides of the small open truck. The road was winding even more now, and the forest had changed to almost all fir and pine, the slopes of the foothills steeper and rockier. Carter studied both sides. A stream ran in a deep bed to the right, the slope rose sharply into the dark conifer forest to the left.

"They'll expect us to go up into the forest for cover," Carter said. "At the next curve I'll pull to the left, but we'll get across to the right into the stream bed. You're armed, Lalita?"

She nodded, and pulled a short, lethal, British Enfield XM-70 from under the front seat.

"Any more?"

"Sait, lift up the rear seat."

The artist did, and drew out two AK-47s. Lalita handed one to Carter, and smiled at Sait Raju. "You keep the other, Sait. Do you know how to use it?"

Raju swallowed hard, but nodded. "I have done my military service."

"Good," Carter said. "Then hang on."

With a curve ahead, Carter stamped hard on the accelerator, skidded the Austin around the curve on two wheels, and screeched to a halt just off the left side of the road.

"Now! Out!"

They leaped out of the still rocking car and raced across the narrow road and down the bank above the stream almost fifty feet below.

"Stop!" Carter hissed. "Back up at the edge and cover the road."

They scrambled up to the edge of the road and lay watching.

The small truck careened around the corner, skidded and slewed across the road as it saw the parked Austin, and slammed on its brakes. Six armed men jumped out.

One of the men was Ahmad Ali Jinnah.

"Pakistanis!" Lalita breathed.

The armed commando who stood beside the Pakistani leader and pointed up the slope through the thick conifer forest was a woman.

"Nasrim Khan," Carter said softly.

"Ah," Lalita whispered in his ear. "I should have known you would find that one. Did you admire the tattoos?"

On the road, Ahmad Ali Jinnah barked orders in Urdu.

"Two of you stay hidden here with the vehicles. Watch for them to come back if they get by us. The rest of you come on. Be careful, that Carter is clever and dangerous."

"So is Lalita Chatterjee," Nasrim Khan said.

The other four men laughed. "For a woman, perhaps," one said.

"For anyone," Nasrim said.

"Nasrim is right, you fools," Jinnah snapped. "Don't underestimate the Chatterjee woman. Now, move!"

The four ran up the slope of the steep hill, short M-16-A1 carbines held at port, and vanished into the trees. The two left behind crouched down in the cover of the Austin.

In the bushes Carter swore. "We'll have to take them out before we can disable their truck and get on our way. Lalita, do you have a knife?"

"Yes, I—"

Raju suddenly whispered in a shaking voice. "Look! They have seen something."

The two men behind the Austin were staring at the road, and then looked up across the road to where Carter and the others watched them. They stood, pointed to the ground, and then whispered to each other. One shook his head. The other insisted. The first pointed up the slope. The second shook his head this time, then suddenly started running across the road straight toward where Carter, Lalita Chatterjee, and Sait Raju lay hidden.

The second Pakistani followed, as if afraid to be left alone.

"Carter!"

"No time! Take them!"

The two Pakistanis were almost to the edge of the stream bank.

Lalita and Carter rose out of the underbrush and squeezed off two short bursts each.

The commandos saw them, stumbled as they tried to dive for the dirt, but were dead in their own spurting blood before they hit the road on their faces.

"Back across the road into the forest!" Carter cried. "Circle right!"

They were too late.

As they raced across the road up ahead of the two parked cars, Jinnah and Nasrim Khan came out of the trees to see what the shooting had been about. The other two Pakistanis appeared farther away behind Jinnah and the small woman.

Jinnah and Nasrim raked the road with bursts from their M-16 carbines.

Carter and Lalita reached the trees and cover.

Sait Raju, running more slowly behind them, didn't make it. The little artist went down, ripped across the chest as if by a giant sewing machine.

"Shit," Carter swore. He raked the road and the distant cars with a hail of fire that sent the Pakistanis scrambling for cover.

"We're almost out of ammunition," Lalita said. "Unless we can get to my car. I've got boxes in the trunk."

"They'll have to reload too. Let's take them now."

Without waiting for Lalita, Carter slipped silently among the trees closer and closer to the vehicles and the four Pakistani commandos hiding behind them. Somewhere behind him he thought he heard Lalita, but he couldn't be sure, as he worked his way around to where he had a clear shot at the two Pakistanis down behind their own truck.

He blew one away with the last rounds in his AK-47.

Ahmad Ali Jinnah and Nasrim Khan ran for the cover of the Austin to take Carter from the side.

A long burst from the British weapon belonging to Lalita Chatterjee sent them sprawling and scrambling on their bellies into the forest again.

The last of the other two suddenly charged straight at where Carter crouched in the shadowed forest, crying *"Al*

Allah Akbar!'' Wilhelmina was steady in Carter's hand as he waited until the man was almost on him, a sudden hope in his eyes. Then Carter fired and the 9mm parabellum slammed the man into the air to sprawl on his back.

Carter moved low to Lalita Chatterjee in the gloom under the thick pines. "They're up the slope maybe a hundred yards now, Nick. They'll wait for us to come to them."

"That'll take too long," Carter said. "We didn't come here to shoot up a few Pakistanis. They know it's two against two, and they won't move on us. Let's get to that camp."

"We'll need poor Sait. He's got the notes of where we're going."

"I'll get him, and you put the truck out of action. Move it fast before they know we're not coming after them."

Lalita silently slashed all four tires on the truck, then cut some wires in the engine. Carter carried the dead Sait Raju to the Austin and deposited him on the back seat.

Moments later they were again on their way to the camp of the Arms of Vengeance.

As they turned the first curve, they saw Ahmad Ali Jinnah and Nasrim Khan come slowly out on the road to stare after them.

—From ARMS OF VENGEANCE
A New Nick Carter Spy Thriller
From Jove in November 1989